W9-CYZ-673

Date: 6/24/20

J GRA 741.5 ALI
Corteggiani, François,
Alice in Wonderland : the
story of the movie in comics

DISNEP

ALICE
in
WONDERLAND

THE STORY OF THE MOVIE IN COMICS

DARK HORSE BOOKS

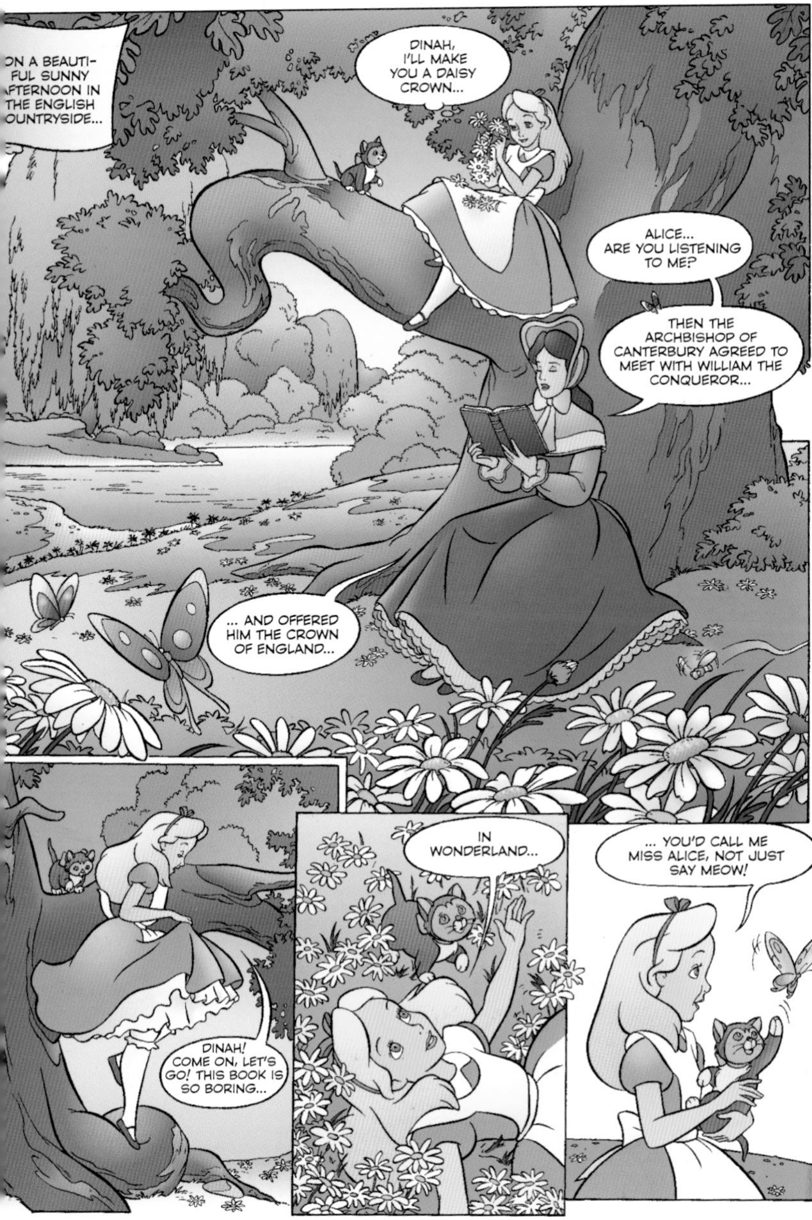
ON A BEAUTI-FUL SUNNY AFTERNOON IN THE ENGLISH COUNTRYSIDE...
DINAH, I'LL MAKE YOU A DAISY CROWN...
ALICE... ARE YOU LISTENING TO ME?
THEN THE ARCHBISHOP OF CANTERBURY AGREED TO MEET WITH WILLIAM THE CONQUEROR...
... AND OFFERED HIM THE CROWN OF ENGLAND...
DINAH! COME ON, LET'S GO! THIS BOOK IS SO BORING...
IN WONDERLAND...
... YOU'D CALL ME MISS ALICE, NOT JUST SAY MEOW!

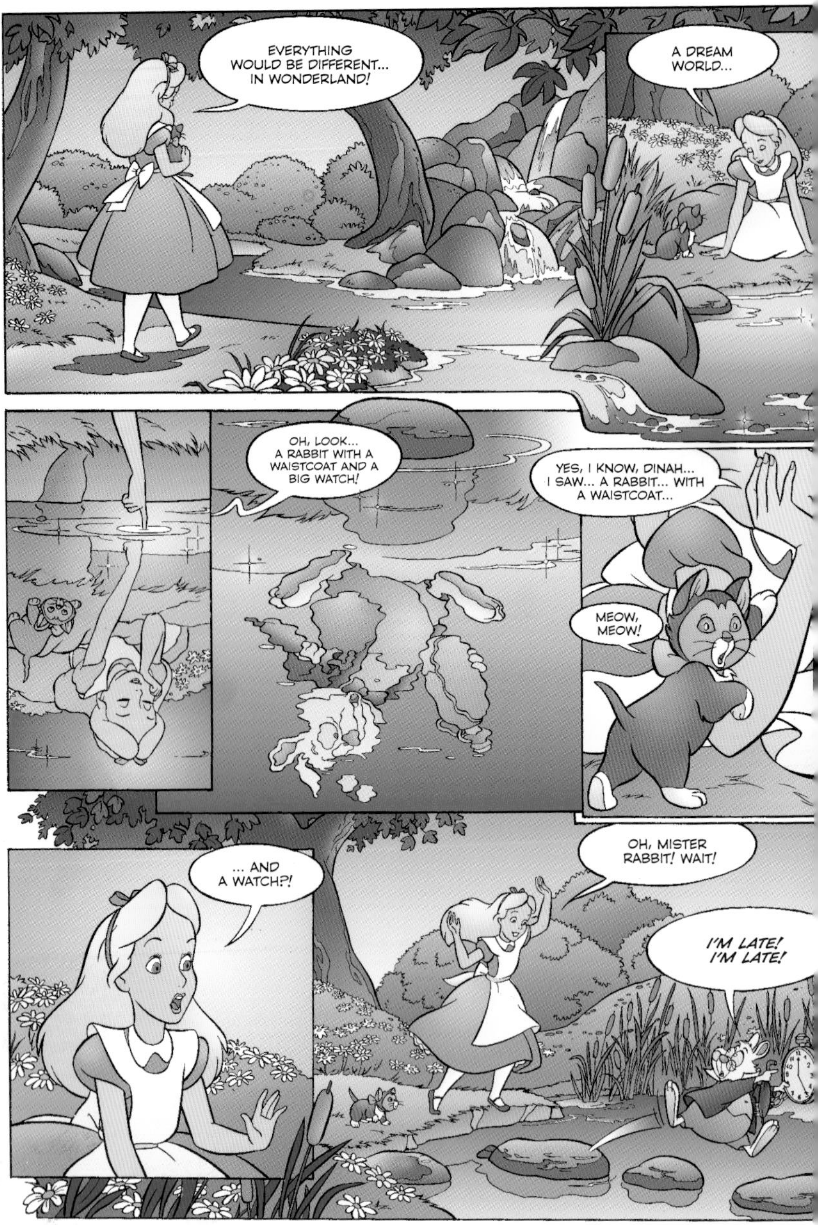
EVERYTHING WOULD BE DIFFERENT... IN WONDERLAND!
A DREAM WORLD...
OH, LOOK... A RABBIT WITH A WAISTCOAT AND A BIG WATCH!
YES, I KNOW, DINAH... I SAW... A RABBIT... WITH A WAISTCOAT...
MEOW, MEOW!
... AND A WATCH?!
OH, MISTER RABBIT! WAIT!
I'M LATE! I'M LATE!

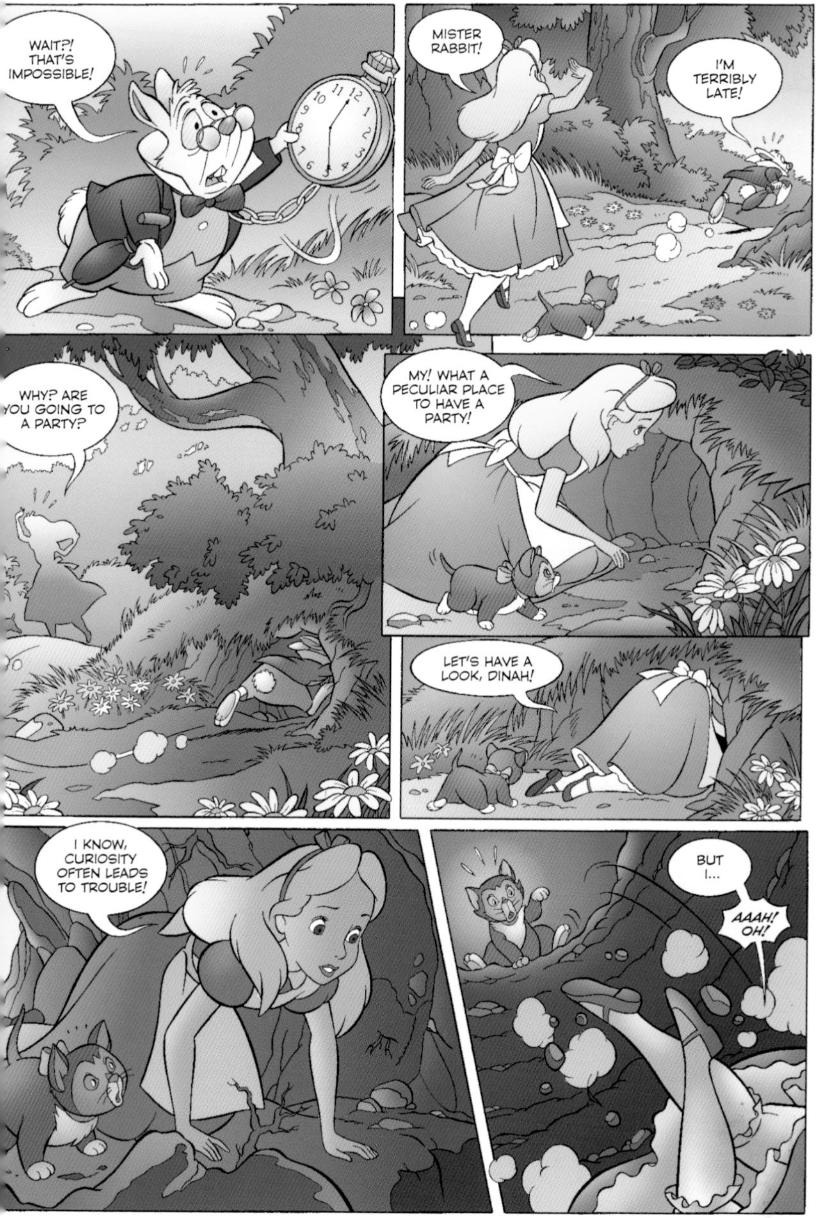
WAIT?! THAT'S IMPOSSIBLE!
MISTER RABBIT!
I'M TERRIBLY LATE!
WHY? ARE YOU GOING TO A PARTY?
MY! WHAT A PECULIAR PLACE TO HAVE A PARTY!
LET'S HAVE A LOOK, DINAH!
I KNOW, CURIOSITY OFTEN LEADS TO TROUBLE!
BUT I...
AAAH! OH!

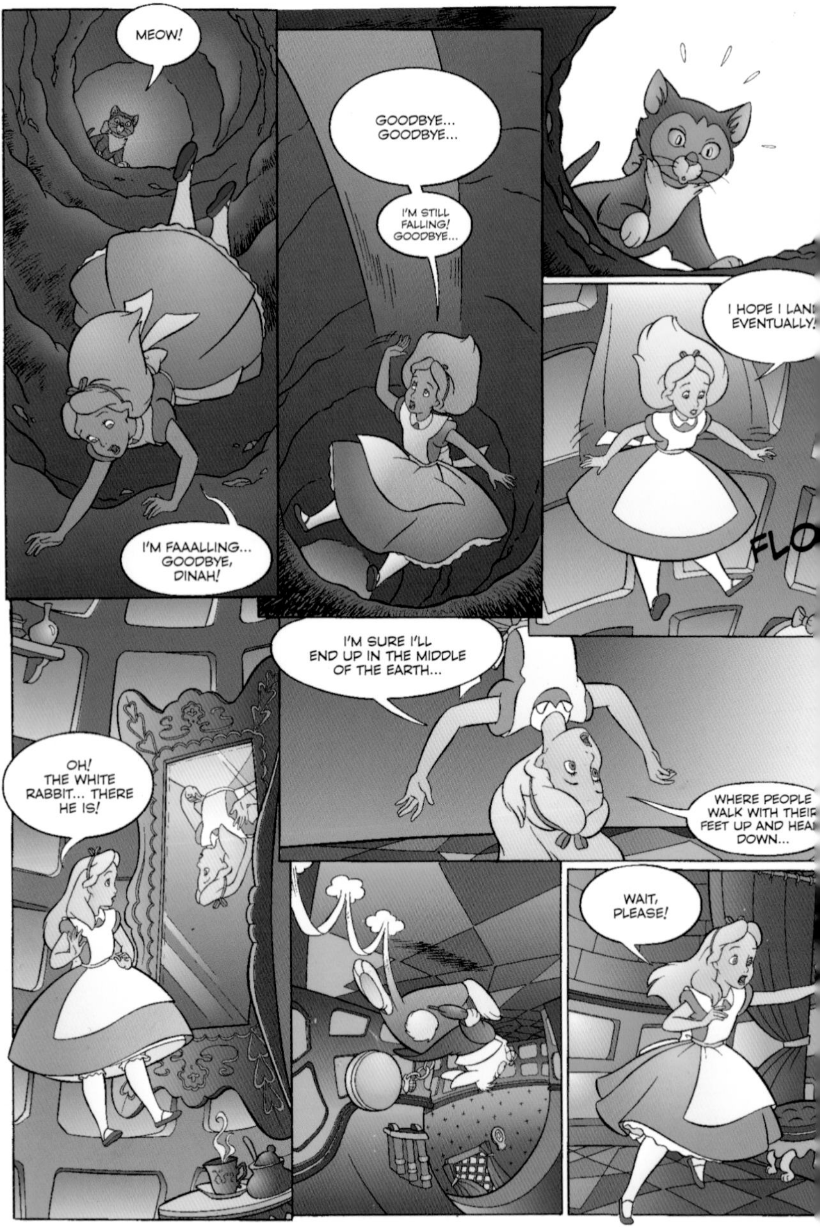
MEOW!
I'M FAAALLING... GOODBYE, DINAH!
GOODBYE... GOODBYE...
I'M STILL FALLING! GOODBYE...
I HOPE I LAN
EVENTUALLY
FLO
I'M SURE I'LL END UP IN THE MIDDLE OF THE EARTH...
WHERE PEOPLE WALK WITH THEI FEET UP AND HEA DOWN...
OH! THE WHITE RABBIT... THERE HE IS!
WAIT, PLEASE!

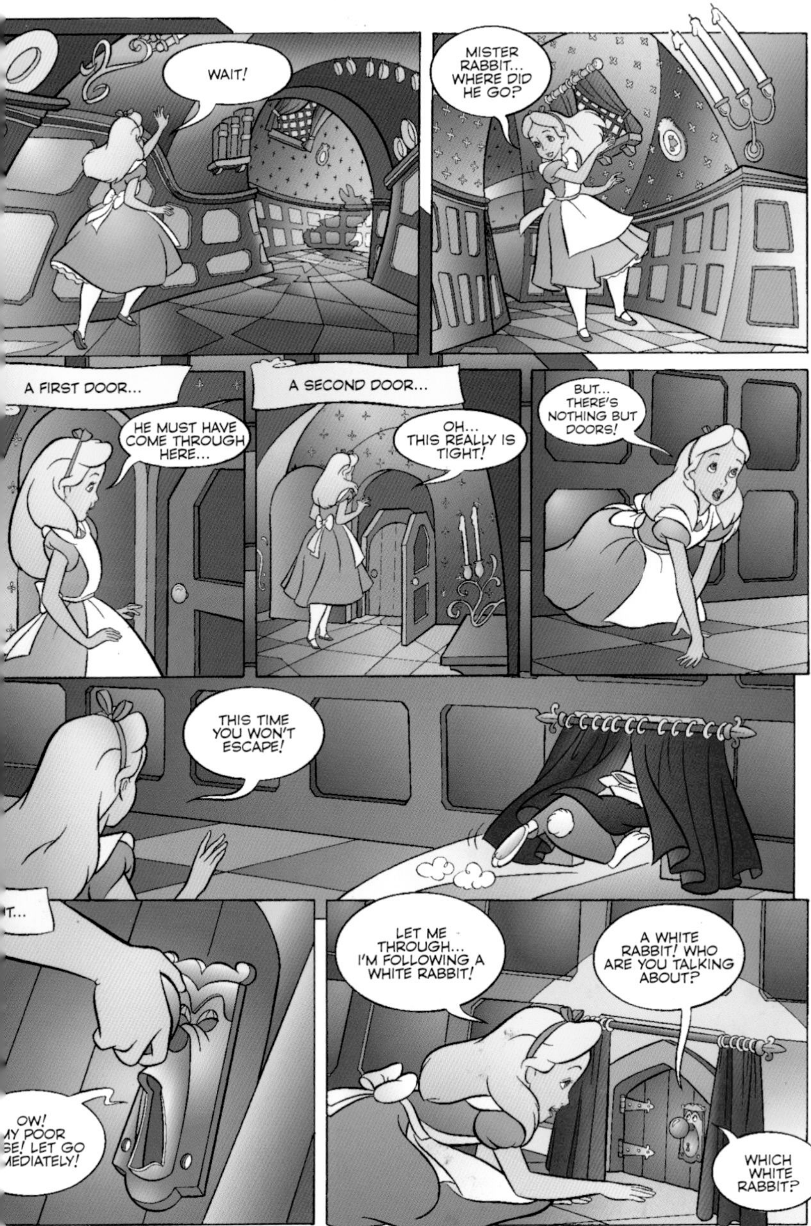
WAIT!
MISTER RABBIT... WHERE DID HE GO?
A FIRST DOOR...
HE MUST HAVE COME THROUGH HERE...
A SECOND DOOR...
OH... THIS REALLY IS TIGHT!
BUT... THERE'S NOTHING BUT DOORS!
THIS TIME YOU WON'T ESCAPE!
T...
OW! MY POOR SE! LET GO MEDIATELY!
LET ME THROUGH... I'M FOLLOWING A WHITE RABBIT!
A WHITE RABBIT! WHO ARE YOU TALKING ABOUT?
WHICH WHITE RABBIT?

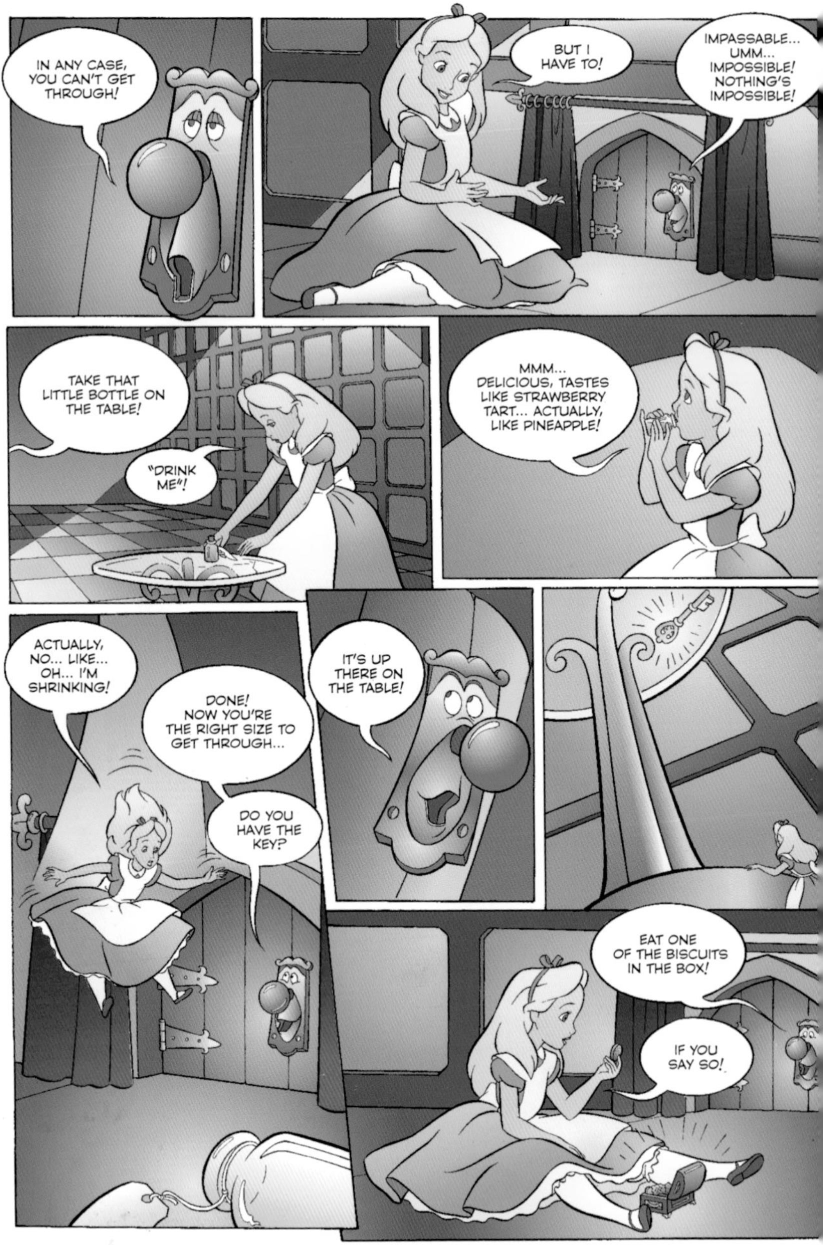
IN ANY CASE, YOU CAN'T GET THROUGH!
BUT I HAVE TO!
IMPASSABLE... UMM... IMPOSSIBLE! NOTHING'S IMPOSSIBLE!
TAKE THAT LITTLE BOTTLE ON THE TABLE!
"DRINK ME"!
MMM... DELICIOUS, TASTES LIKE STRAWBERRY TART... ACTUALLY, LIKE PINEAPPLE!
ACTUALLY, NO... LIKE... OH... I'M SHRINKING!
DONE! NOW YOU'RE THE RIGHT SIZE TO GET THROUGH...
DO YOU HAVE THE KEY?
IT'S UP THERE ON THE TABLE!
EAT ONE OF THE BISCUITS IN THE BOX!
IF YOU SAY SO!

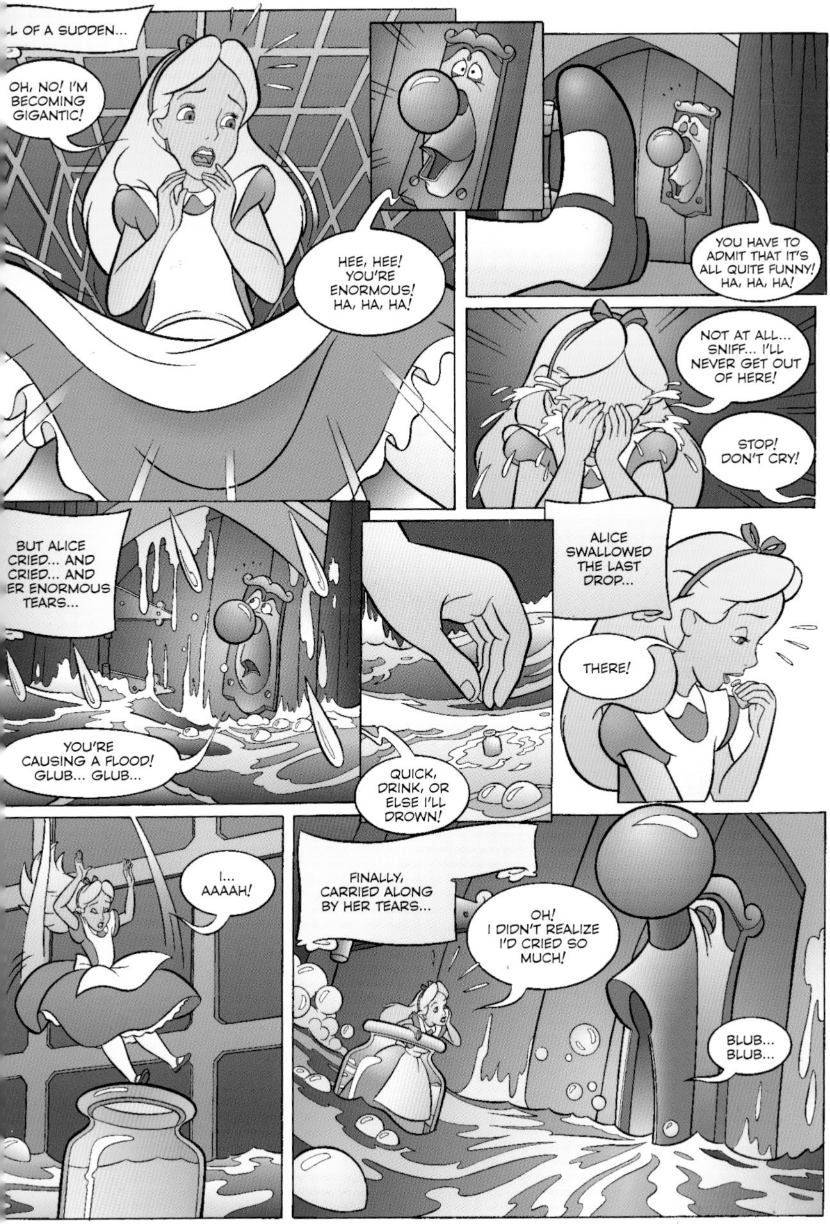

L OF A SUDDEN...
OH, NO! I'M BECOMING GIGANTIC!
HEE, HEE! YOU'RE ENORMOUS! HA, HA, HA!
YOU HAVE TO ADMIT THAT IT'S ALL QUITE FUNNY! HA, HA, HA!
NOT AT ALL... SNIFF... I'LL NEVER GET OUT OF HERE!
STOP! DON'T CRY!
BUT ALICE CRIED... AND CRIED... AND ER ENORMOUS TEARS...
YOU'RE CAUSING A FLOOD! GLUB... GLUB...
QUICK, DRINK, OR ELSE I'LL DROWN!
ALICE SWALLOWED THE LAST DROP...
THERE!
I... AAAAH!
FINALLY, CARRIED ALONG BY HER TEARS...
OH! I DIDN'T REALIZE I'D CRIED SO MUCH!
BLUB... BLUB...

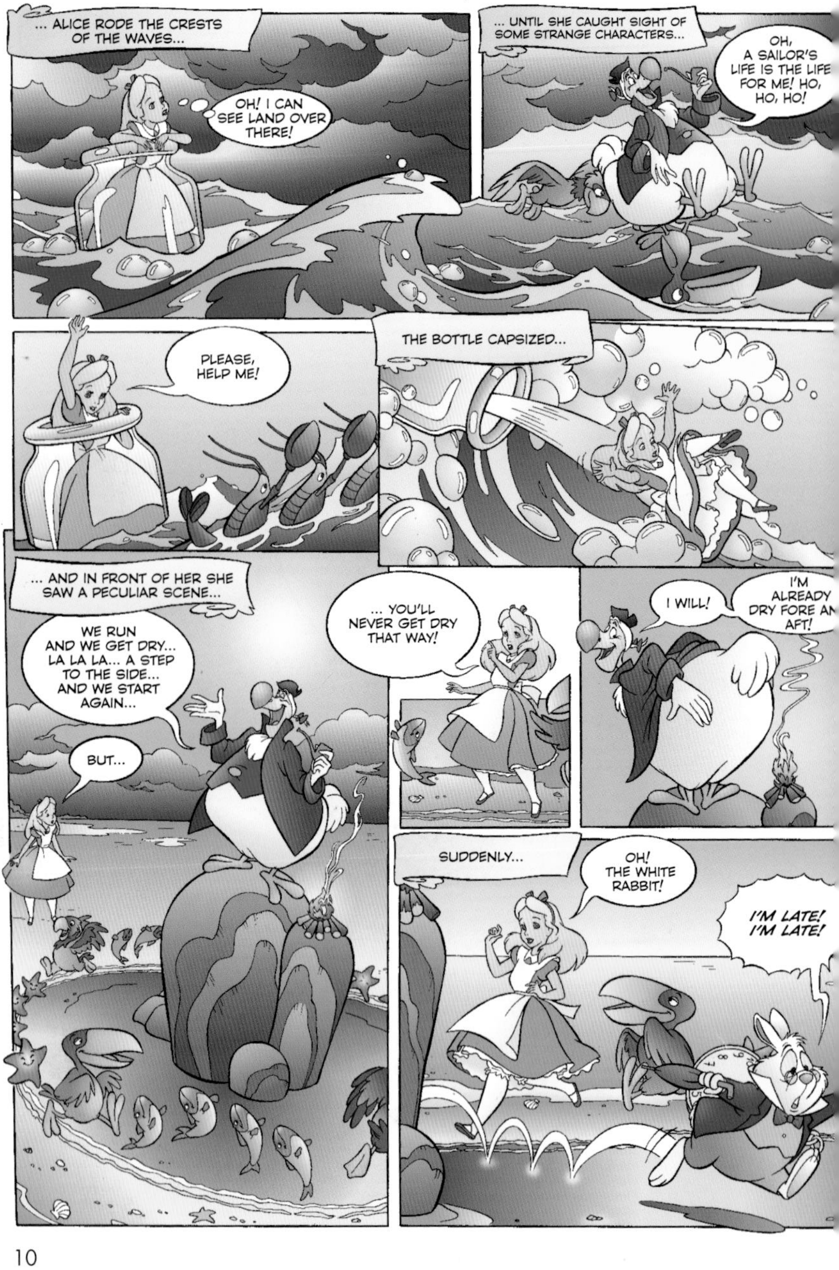
... ALICE RODE THE CRESTS OF THE WAVES...
OH! I CAN SEE LAND OVER THERE!
... UNTIL SHE CAUGHT SIGHT OF SOME STRANGE CHARACTERS...
OH, A SAILOR'S LIFE IS THE LIFE FOR ME! HO, HO, HO!
PLEASE, HELP ME!
THE BOTTLE CAPSIZED...
... AND IN FRONT OF HER SHE SAW A PECULIAR SCENE...
WE RUN AND WE GET DRY... LA LA LA... A STEP TO THE SIDE... AND WE START AGAIN...
BUT...
... YOU'LL NEVER GET DRY THAT WAY!
I WILL!
I'M ALREADY DRY FORE AN AFT!
SUDDENLY...
OH! THE WHITE RABBIT!
I'M LATE! I'M LATE!

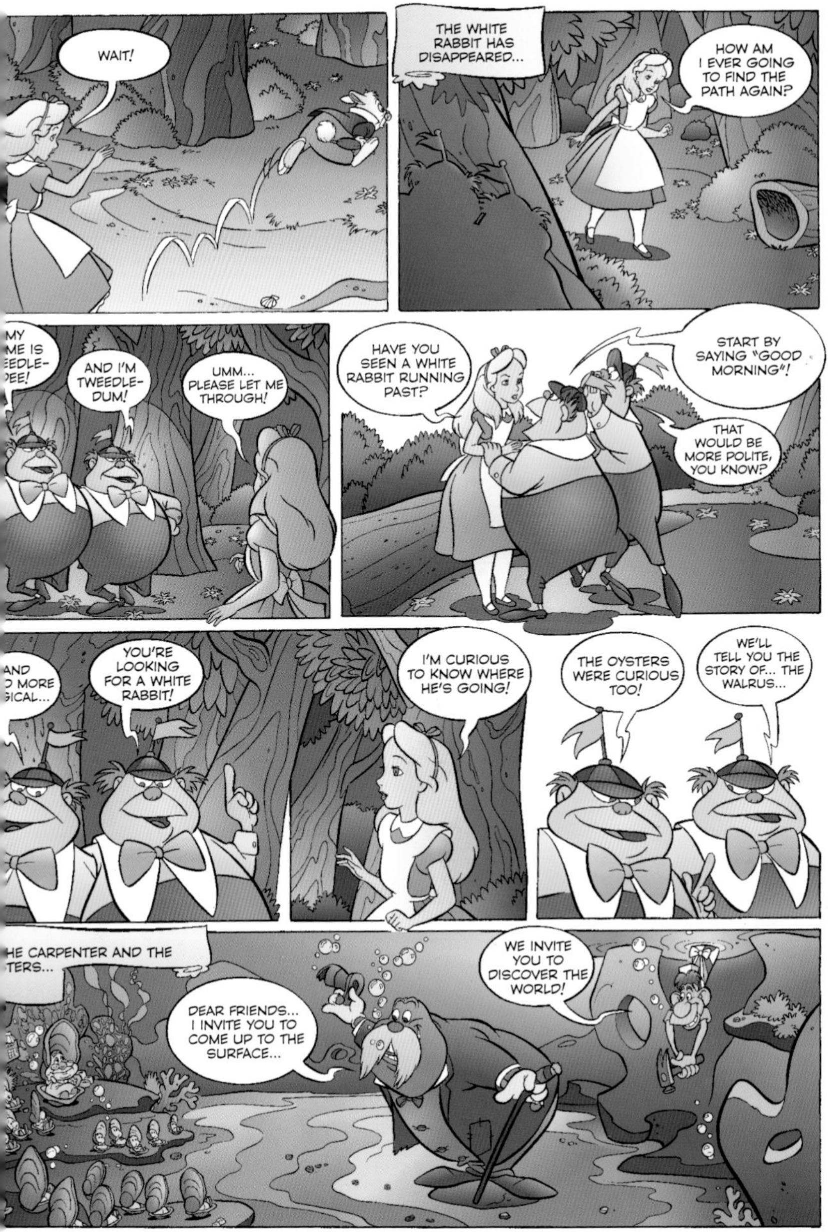
WAIT!
THE WHITE RABBIT HAS DISAPPEARED...
HOW AM I EVER GOING TO FIND THE PATH AGAIN?
MY ME IS EEDLE- DEE!
AND I'M TWEEDLE-DUM!
UMM... PLEASE LET ME THROUGH!
HAVE YOU SEEN A WHITE RABBIT RUNNING PAST?
START BY SAYING "GOOD MORNING"!
THAT WOULD BE MORE POLITE, YOU KNOW?
AND MORE GICAL...
YOU'RE LOOKING FOR A WHITE RABBIT!
I'M CURIOUS TO KNOW WHERE HE'S GOING!
THE OYSTERS WERE CURIOUS TOO!
WE'LL TELL YOU THE STORY OF... THE WALRUS...
HE CARPENTER AND THE TERS...
DEAR FRIENDS... I INVITE YOU TO COME UP TO THE SURFACE...
WE INVITE YOU TO DISCOVER THE WORLD!

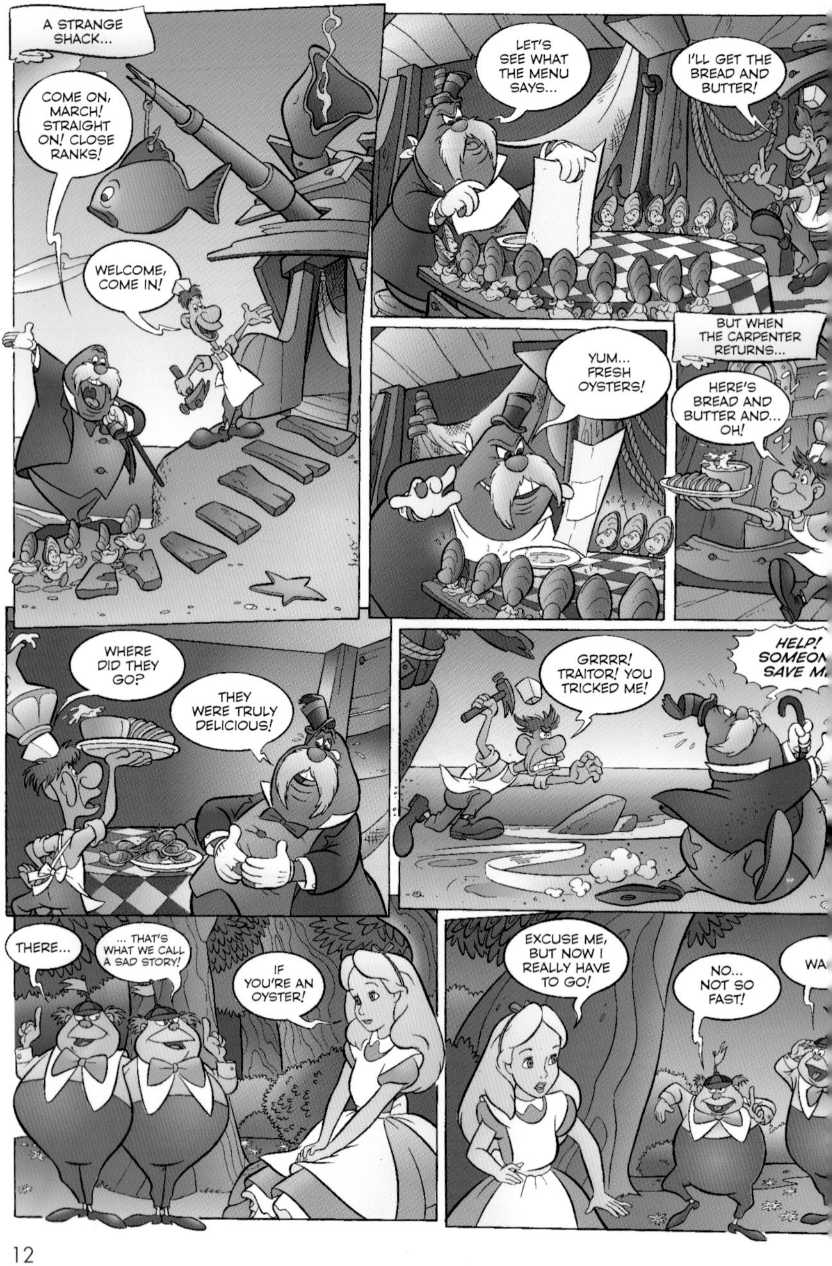
A STRANGE SHACK...
COME ON, MARCH! STRAIGHT ON! CLOSE RANKS!
WELCOME, COME IN!
LET'S SEE WHAT THE MENU SAYS...
I'LL GET THE BREAD AND BUTTER!
YUM... FRESH OYSTERS!
BUT WHEN THE CARPENTER RETURNS...
HERE'S BREAD AND BUTTER AND... OH!
WHERE DID THEY GO?
THEY WERE TRULY DELICIOUS!
GRRRR! TRAITOR! YOU TRICKED ME!
THERE...
... THAT'S WHAT WE CALL A SAD STORY!
IF YOU'RE AN OYSTER!
EXCUSE ME, BUT NOW I REALLY HAVE TO GO!
NO... NOT SO FAST!

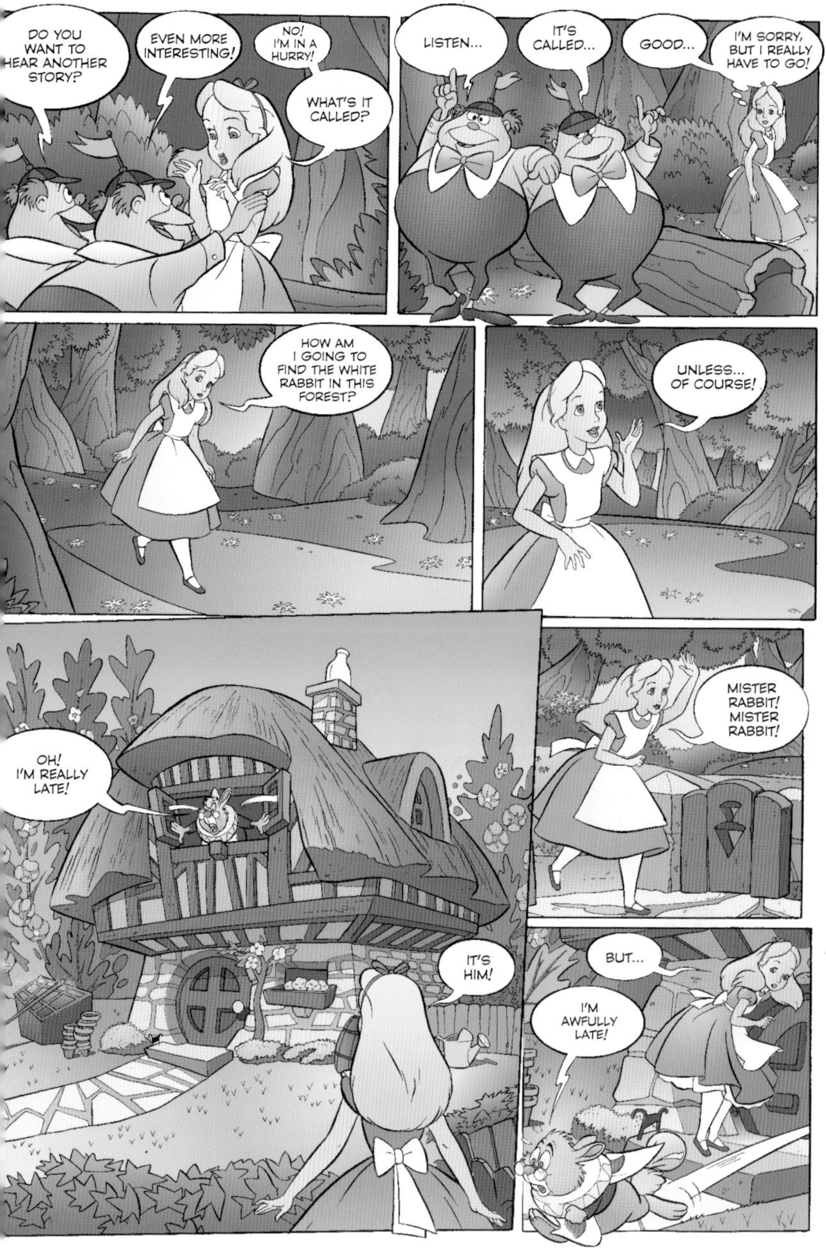
DO YOU WANT TO HEAR ANOTHER STORY?
EVEN MORE INTERESTING!
NO! I'M IN A HURRY!
WHAT'S IT CALLED?
LISTEN...
IT'S CALLED...
GOOD...
I'M SORRY, BUT I REALLY HAVE TO GO!
HOW AM I GOING TO FIND THE WHITE RABBIT IN THIS FOREST?
UNLESS... OF COURSE!
OH! I'M REALLY LATE!
IT'S HIM!
MISTER RABBIT! MISTER RABBIT!
BUT...
I'M AWFULLY LATE!

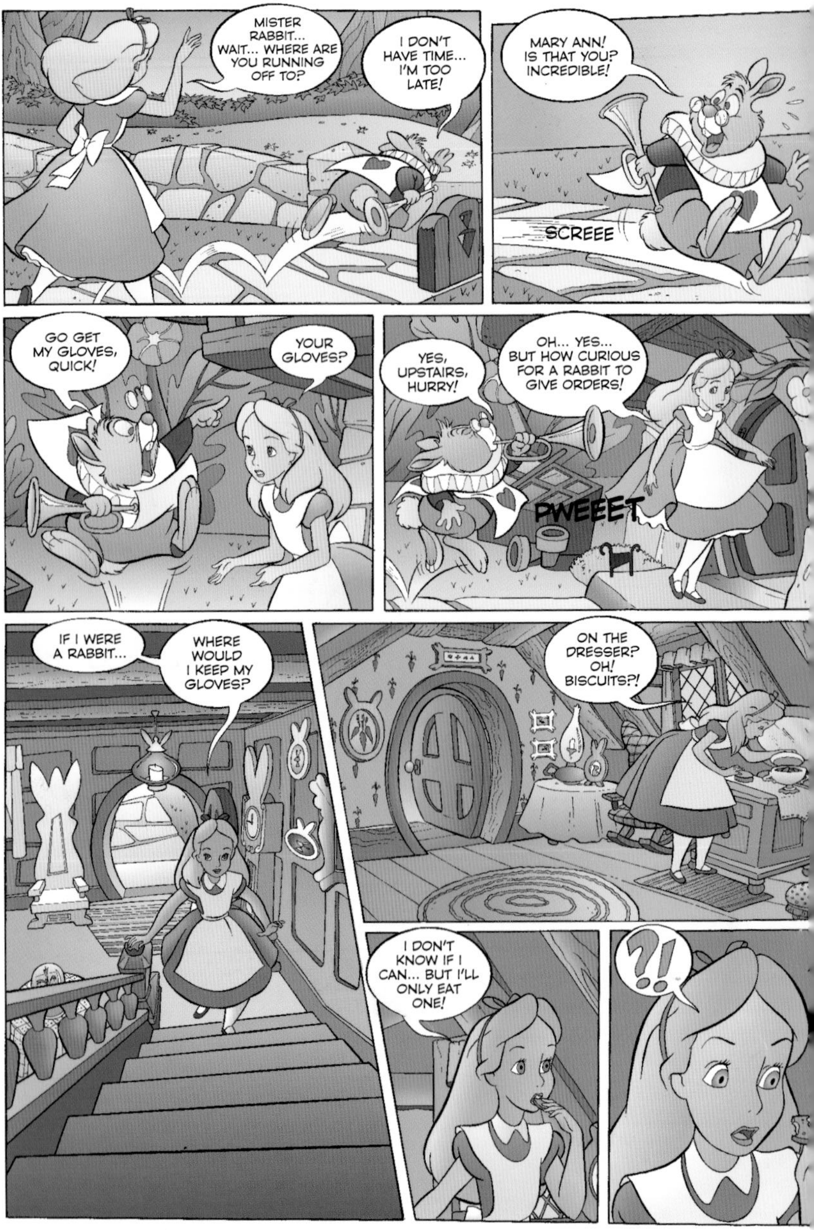
MISTER RABBIT... WAIT... WHERE ARE YOU RUNNING OFF TO?
I DON'T HAVE TIME... I'M TOO LATE!
MARY ANN! IS THAT YOU? INCREDIBLE!
SCREEE
GO GET MY GLOVES, QUICK!
YOUR GLOVES?
YES, UPSTAIRS, HURRY!
OH... YES... BUT HOW CURIOUS FOR A RABBIT TO GIVE ORDERS!
PWEEET
IF I WERE A RABBIT...
WHERE WOULD I KEEP MY GLOVES?
ON THE DRESSER? OH! BISCUITS?!
I DON'T KNOW IF I CAN... BUT I'LL ONLY EAT ONE!
?!

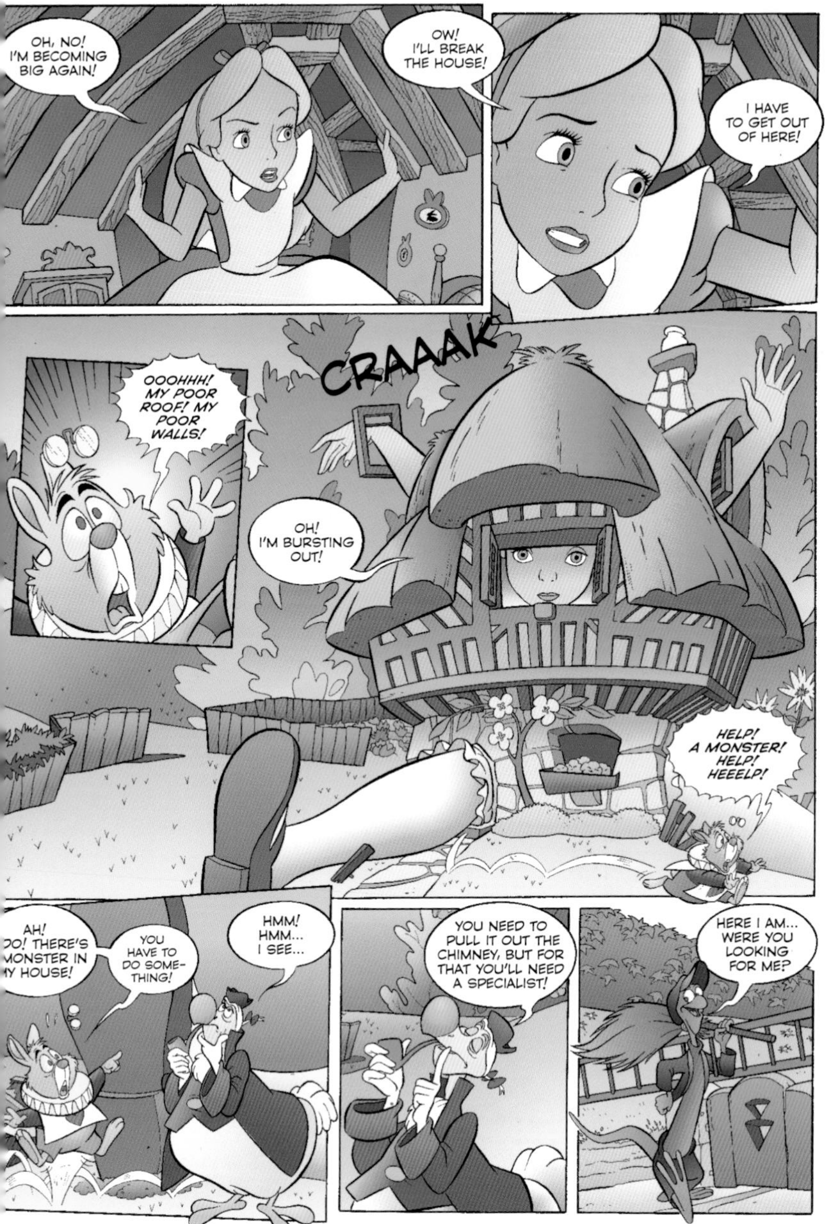
OH, NO! I'M BECOMING BIG AGAIN!
OW! I'LL BREAK THE HOUSE!
I HAVE TO GET OUT OF HERE!
CRAAAK
OOOHHH! MY POOR ROOF! MY POOR WALLS!
OH! I'M BURSTING OUT!
HELP! A MONSTER! HELP! HEEELP!
AH! OO! THERE'S MONSTER IN Y HOUSE!
YOU HAVE TO DO SOME-THING!
HMM! HMM... I SEE...
YOU NEED TO PULL IT OUT THE CHIMNEY, BUT FOR THAT YOU'LL NEED A SPECIALIST!
HERE I AM... WERE YOU LOOKING FOR ME?

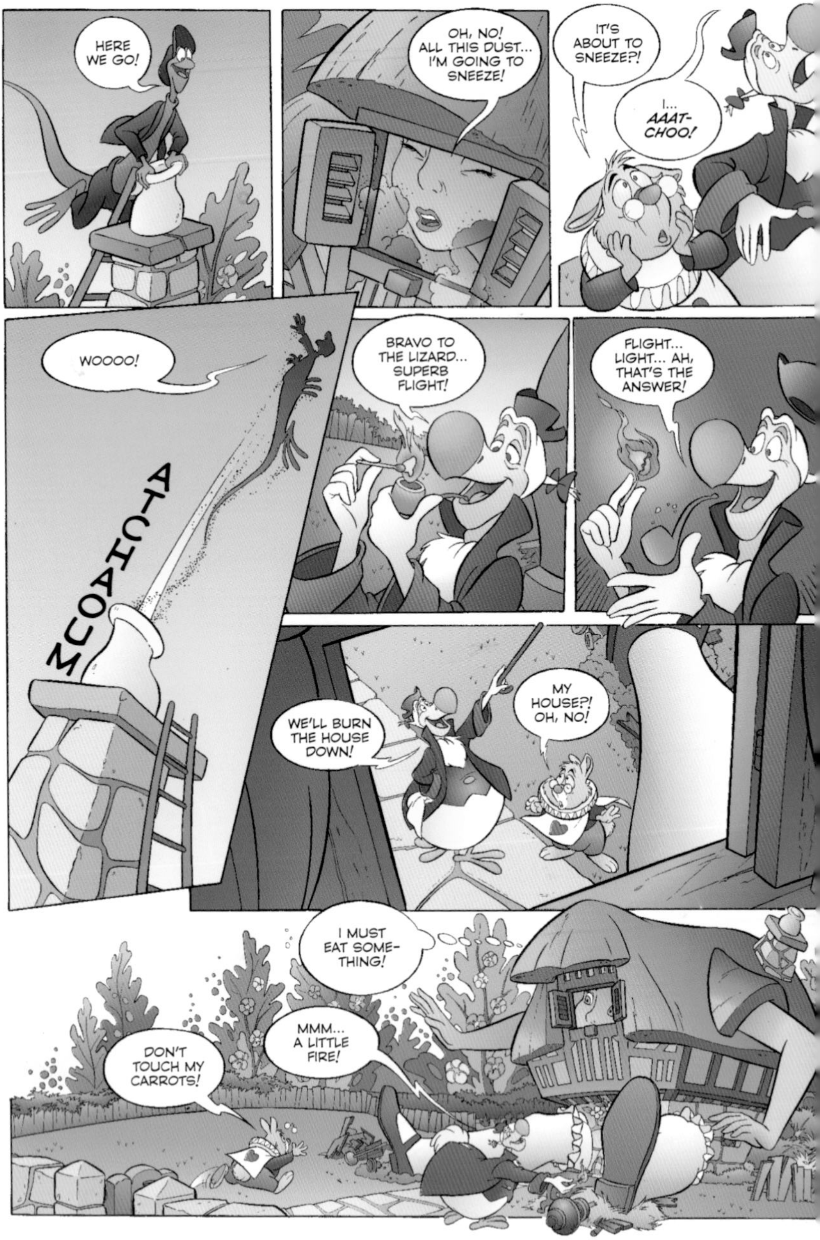
HERE WE GO!
OH, NO! ALL THIS DUST... I'M GOING TO SNEEZE!
IT'S ABOUT TO SNEEZE?!
I... AAAT-CHOO!
WOOOO!
ATCHAOUM
BRAVO TO THE LIZARD... SUPERB FLIGHT!
FLIGHT... LIGHT... AH, THAT'S THE ANSWER!
WE'LL BURN THE HOUSE DOWN!
MY HOUSE?! OH, NO!
I MUST EAT SOME-THING!
MMM... A LITTLE FIRE!
DON'T TOUCH MY CARROTS!

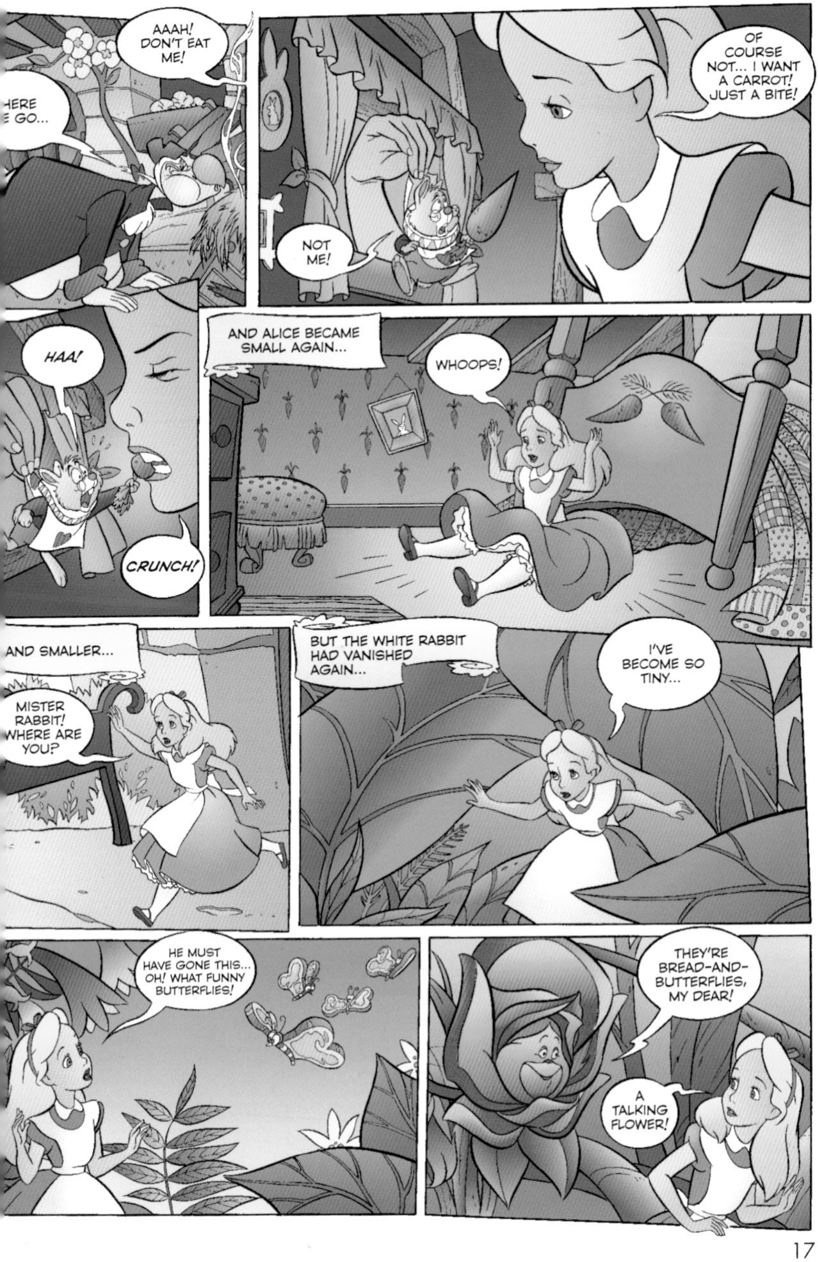
AAAH! DON'T EAT ME!
HERE
E GO...
OF COURSE NOT... I WANT A CARROT! JUST A BITE!
NOT ME!
HAA!
CRUNCH!
AND ALICE BECAME SMALL AGAIN...
WHOOPS!
AND SMALLER...
MISTER RABBIT! WHERE ARE YOU?
BUT THE WHITE RABBIT HAD VANISHED AGAIN...
I'VE BECOME SO TINY...
HE MUST HAVE GONE THIS... OH! WHAT FUNNY BUTTERFLIES!
THEY'RE BREAD-AND-BUTTERFLIES, MY DEAR!
A TALKING FLOWER!

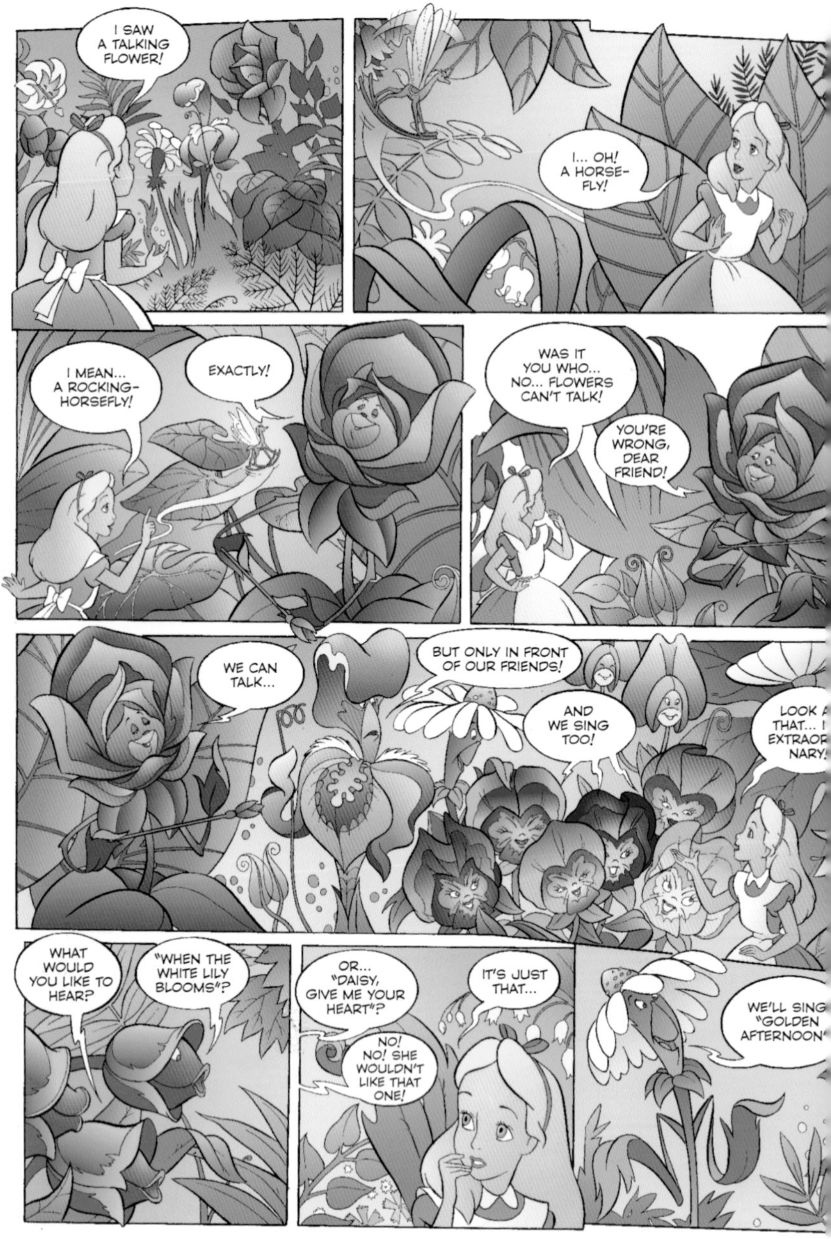
I SAW A TALKING FLOWER!
I... OH! A HORSE-FLY!
I MEAN... A ROCKING-HORSEFLY!
EXACTLY!
WAS IT YOU WHO... NO... FLOWERS CAN'T TALK!
YOU'RE WRONG, DEAR FRIEND!
WE CAN TALK...
BUT ONLY IN FRONT OF OUR FRIENDS!
AND WE SING TOO!
LOOK A THAT... I EXTRAOR NARY!
WHAT WOULD YOU LIKE TO HEAR?
"WHEN THE WHITE LILY BLOOMS"?
OR... "DAISY, GIVE ME YOUR HEART"?
NO! NO! SHE WOULDN'T LIKE THAT ONE!
IT'S JUST THAT...
WE'LL SING "GOLDEN AFTERNOON

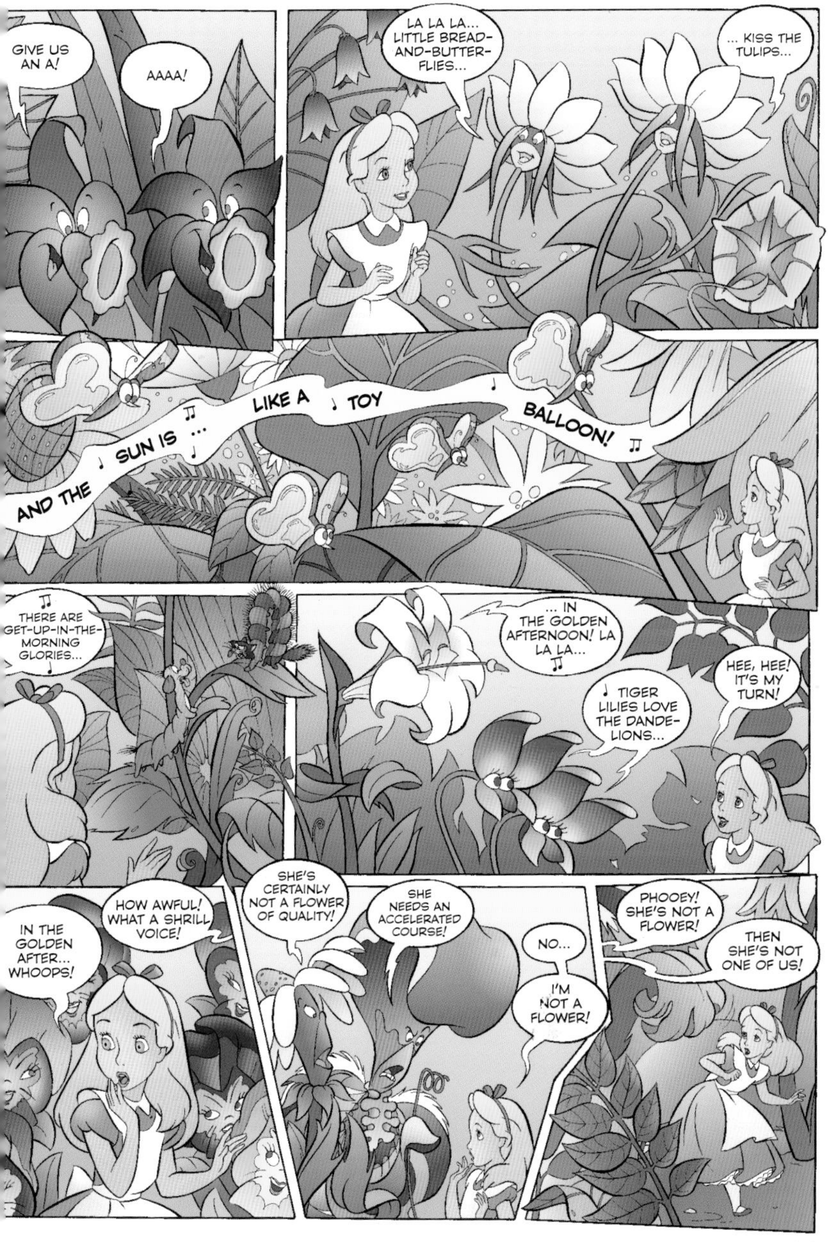
GIVE US AN A!
AAAA!
LA LA LA... LITTLE BREAD-AND-BUTTER-FLIES...
... KISS THE TULIPS...
AND THE SUN IS ... LIKE A TOY BALLOON!
THERE ARE GET-UP-IN-THE-MORNING GLORIES...
... IN THE GOLDEN AFTERNOON! LA LA LA...
TIGER LILIES LOVE THE DANDE-LIONS...
HEE, HEE! IT'S MY TURN!
IN THE GOLDEN AFTER... WHOOPS!
HOW AWFUL! WHAT A SHRILL VOICE!
SHE'S CERTAINLY NOT A FLOWER OF QUALITY!
SHE NEEDS AN ACCELERATED COURSE!
NO...
I'M NOT A FLOWER!
PHOOEY! SHE'S NOT A FLOWER!
THEN SHE'S NOT ONE OF US!

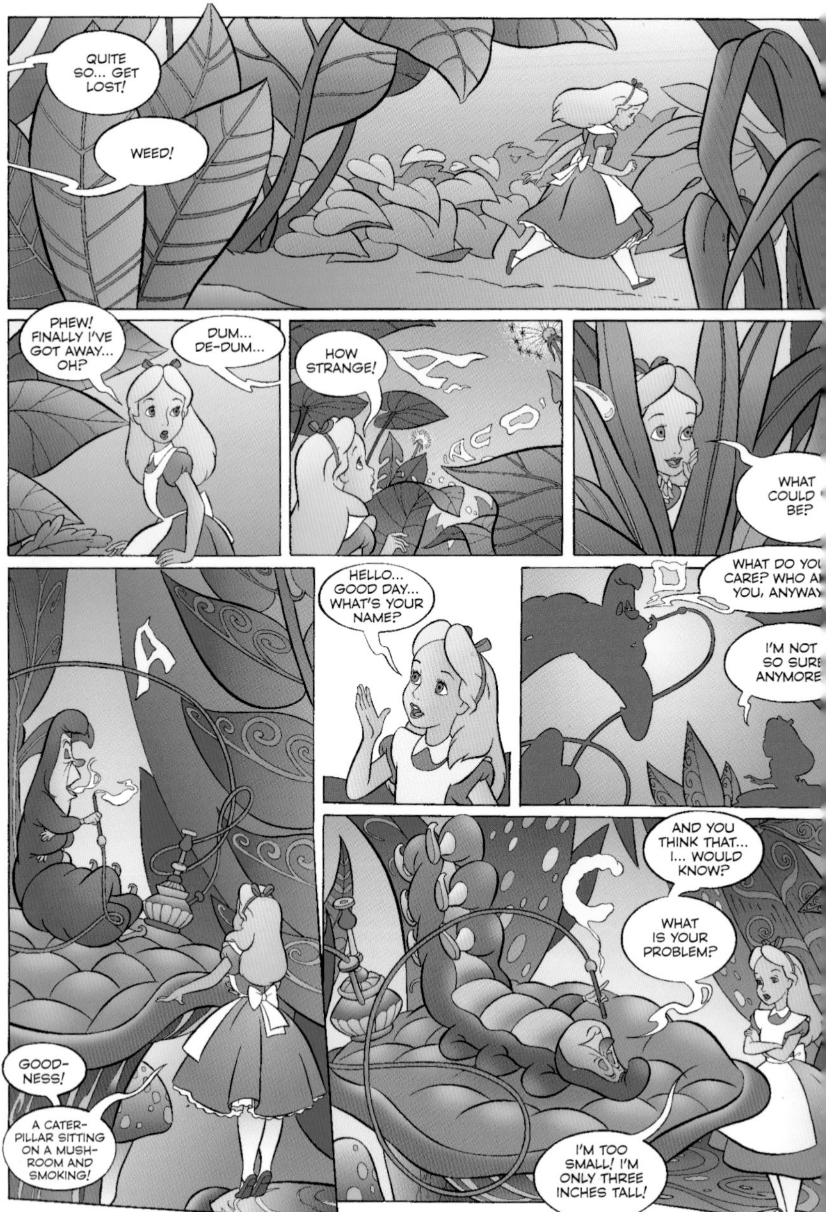

QUITE SO... GET LOST!
WEED!
PHEW! FINALLY I'VE GOT AWAY... OH?
DUM... DE-DUM...
HOW STRANGE!
WHAT COULD BE?
GOODNESS!
A CATERPILLAR SITTING ON A MUSHROOM AND SMOKING!
HELLO... GOOD DAY... WHAT'S YOUR NAME?
WHAT DO YO CARE? WHO A YOU, ANYWAY
I'M NOT SO SURE ANYMORE
AND YOU THINK THAT... I... WOULD KNOW?
WHAT IS YOUR PROBLEM?
I'M TOO SMALL! I'M ONLY THREE INCHES TALL!

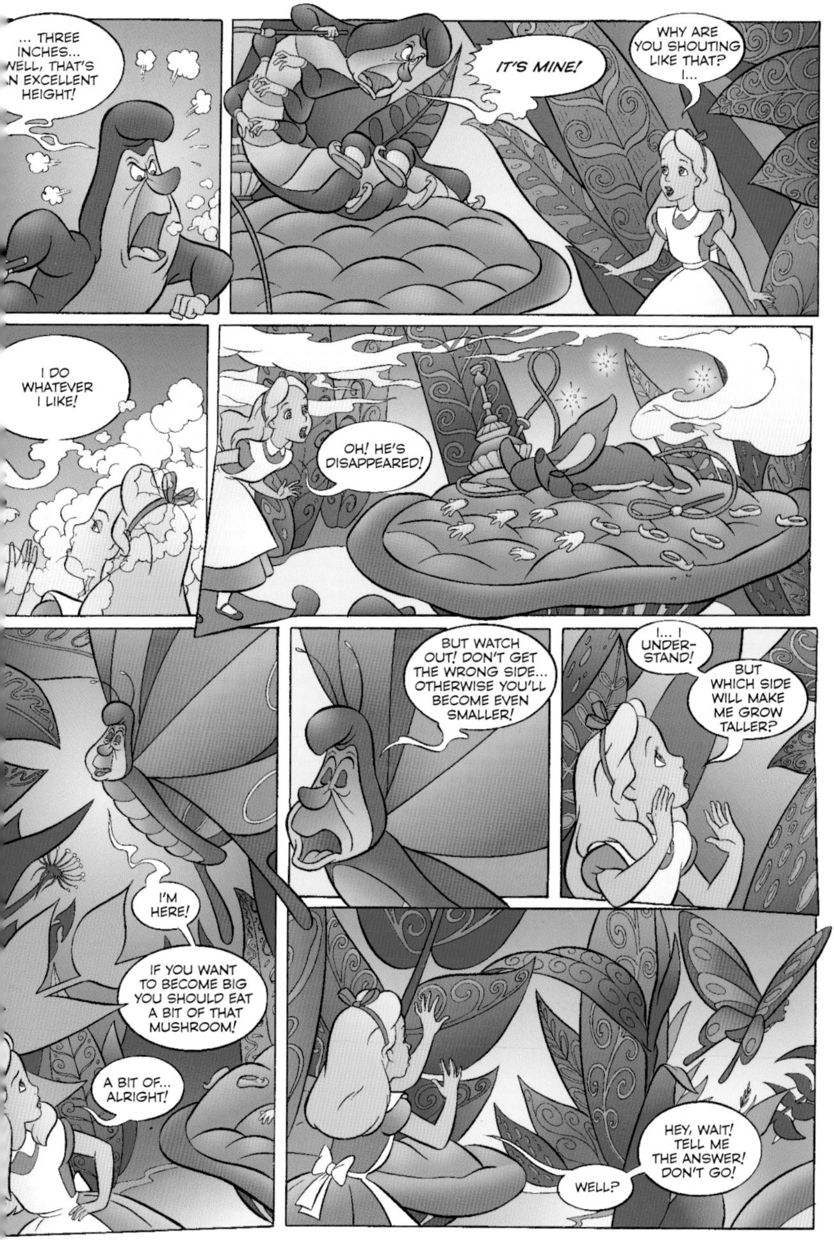
... THREE INCHES... WELL, THAT'S AN EXCELLENT HEIGHT!
IT'S MINE!
WHY ARE YOU SHOUTING LIKE THAT? I...
I DO WHATEVER I LIKE!
OH! HE'S DISAPPEARED!
I'M HERE!
IF YOU WANT TO BECOME BIG YOU SHOULD EAT A BIT OF THAT MUSHROOM!
A BIT OF... ALRIGHT!
BUT WATCH OUT! DON'T GET THE WRONG SIDE... OTHERWISE YOU'LL BECOME EVEN SMALLER!
I... I UNDER-STAND!
BUT WHICH SIDE WILL MAKE ME GROW TALLER?
WELL?
HEY, WAIT! TELL ME THE ANSWER! DON'T GO!

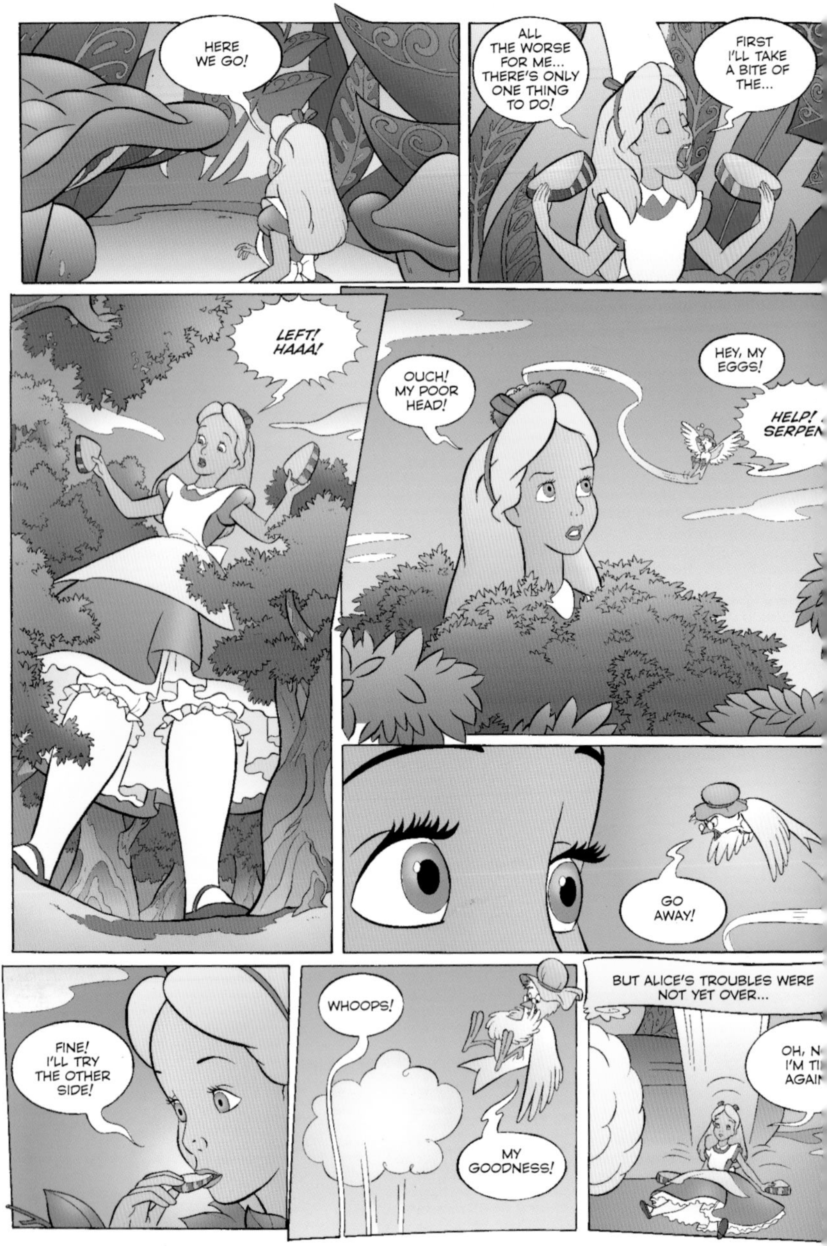
HERE WE GO!
ALL THE WORSE FOR ME... THERE'S ONLY ONE THING TO DO!
FIRST I'LL TAKE A BITE OF THE...
LEFT! HAAA!
OUCH! MY POOR HEAD!
HEY, MY EGGS!
HELP!
GO AWAY!
FINE! I'LL TRY THE OTHER SIDE!
WHOOPS!
MY GOODNESS!
BUT ALICE'S TROUBLES WERE NOT YET OVER...

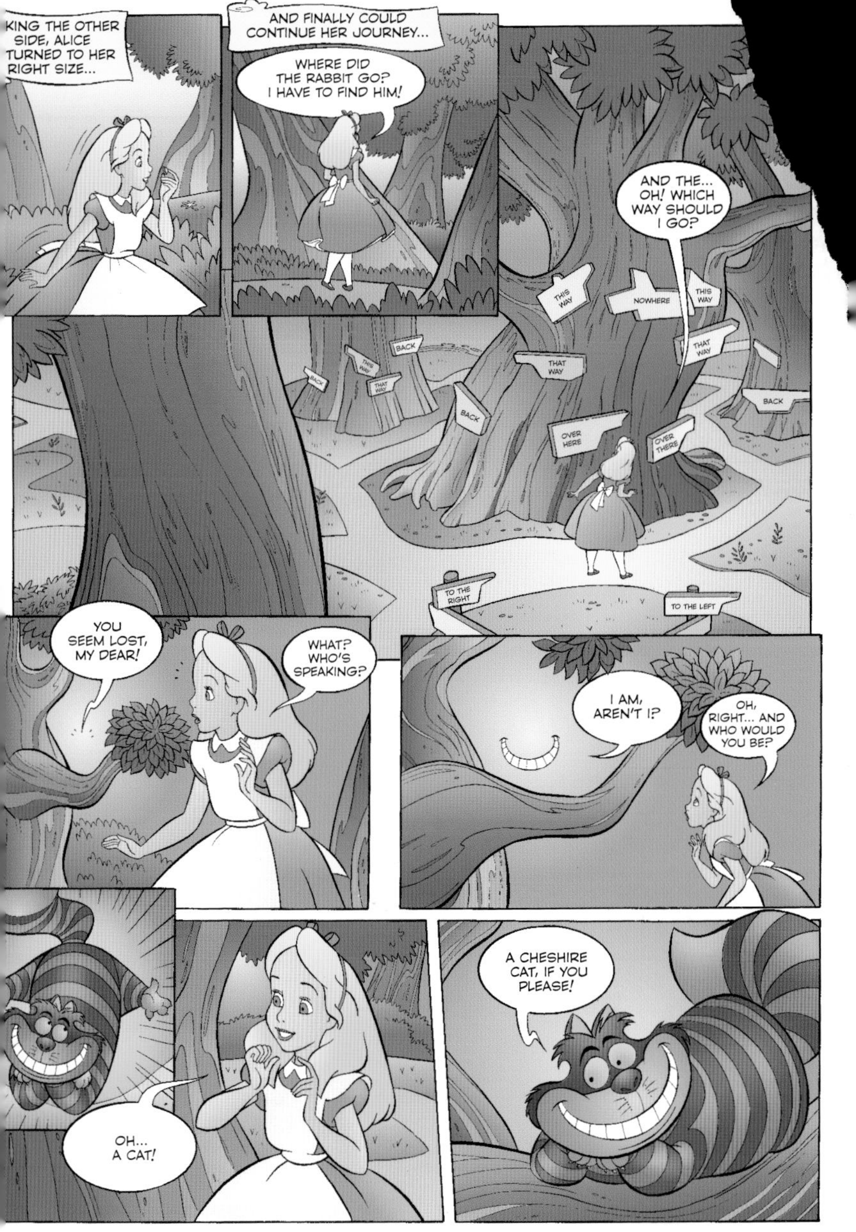
KING THE OTHER SIDE, ALICE TURNED TO HER RIGHT SIZE...
AND FINALLY COULD CONTINUE HER JOURNEY...
WHERE DID THE RABBIT GO? I HAVE TO FIND HIM!
AND THE... OH! WHICH WAY SHOULD I GO?
THIS WAY
NOWHERE
THIS WAY
BACK
THIS WAY
THAT WAY
BACK
THAT WAY
THAT WAY
BACK
BACK
OVER HERE
OVER THERE
TO THE RIGHT
TO THE LEFT
YOU SEEM LOST, MY DEAR!
WHAT? WHO'S SPEAKING?
I AM, AREN'T I?
OH, RIGHT... AND WHO WOULD YOU BE?
OH... A CAT!
A CHESHIRE CAT, IF YOU PLEASE!

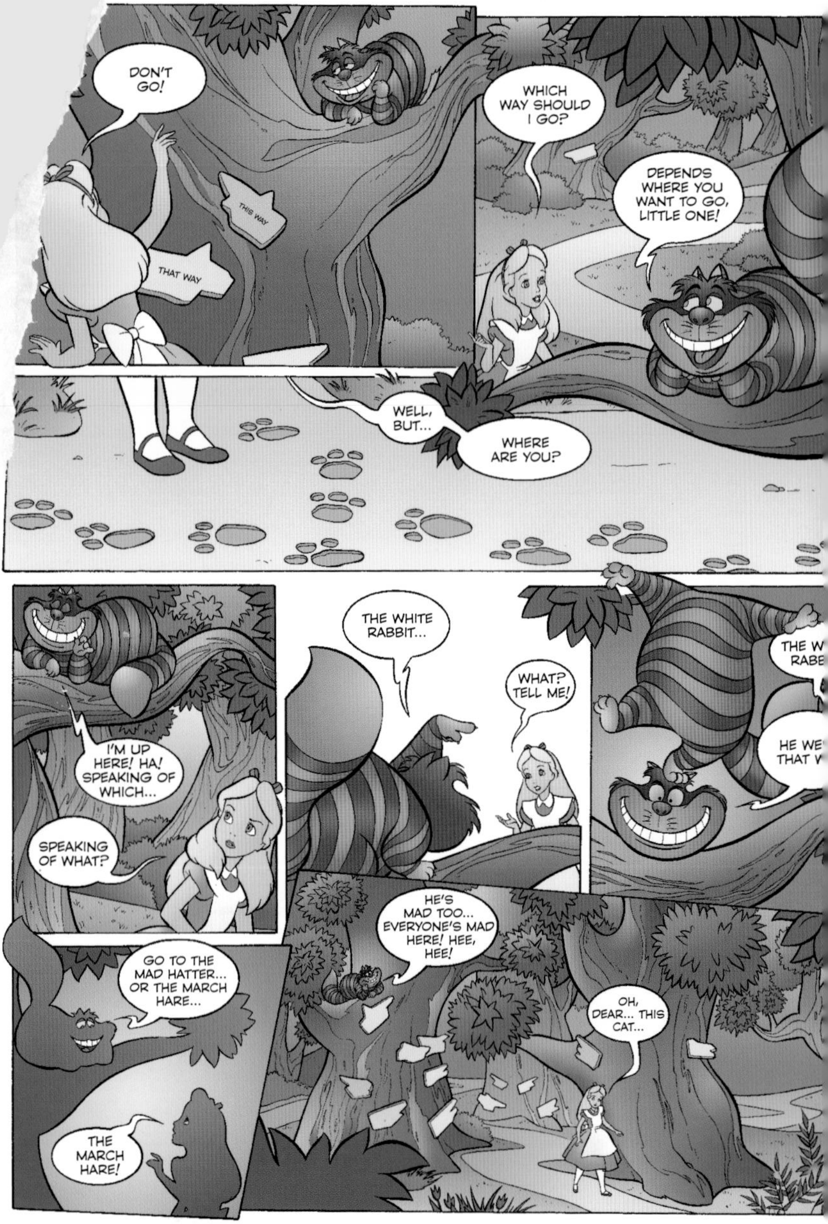
DON'T GO!
THIS WAY
THAT WAY
WHICH WAY SHOULD I GO?
DEPENDS WHERE YOU WANT TO GO, LITTLE ONE!
WELL, BUT...
WHERE ARE YOU?
I'M UP HERE! HA! SPEAKING OF WHICH...
SPEAKING OF WHAT?
THE WHITE RABBIT...
WHAT? TELL ME!
GO TO THE MAD HATTER... OR THE MARCH HARE...
THE MARCH HARE!
HE'S MAD TOO... EVERYONE'S MAD HERE! HEE, HEE!
OH, DEAR... THIS CAT...

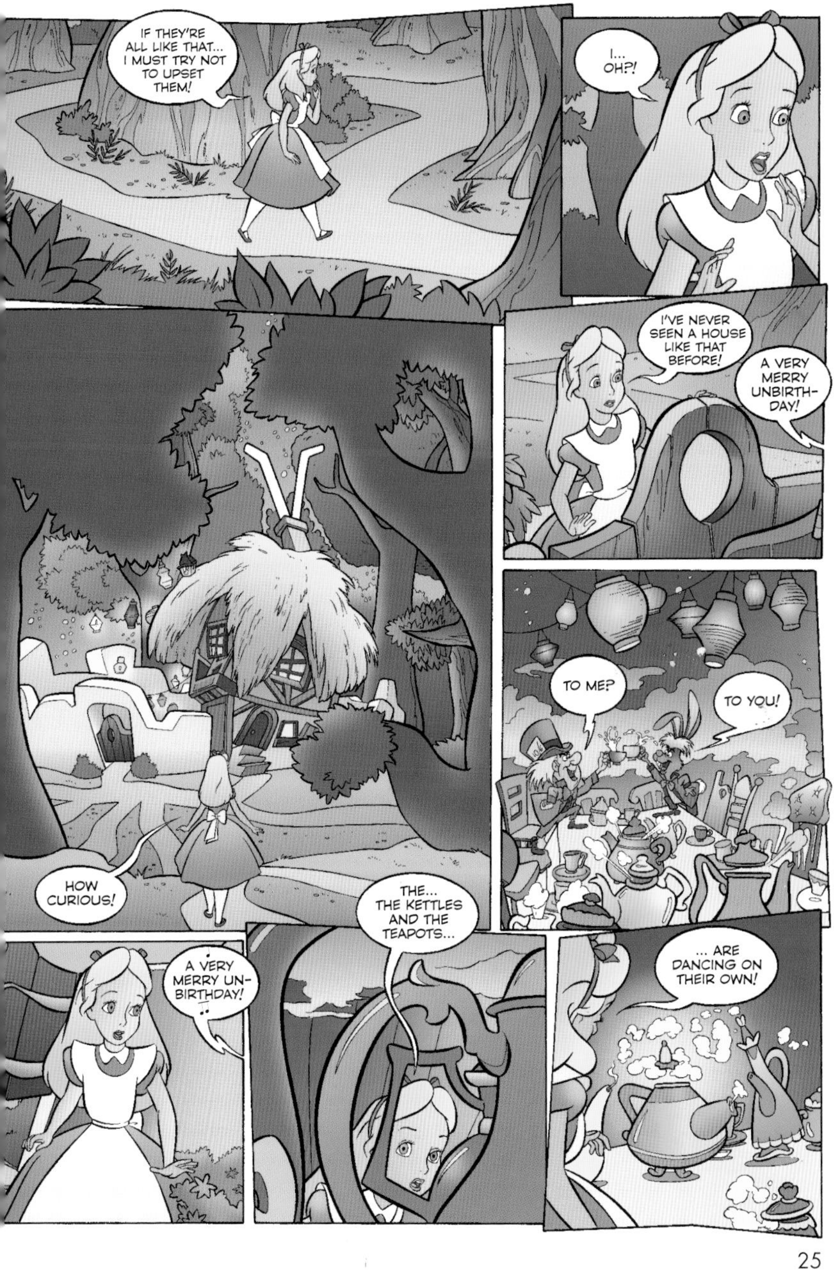
IF THEY'RE ALL LIKE THAT... I MUST TRY NOT TO UPSET THEM!
I... OH?!
HOW CURIOUS!
I'VE NEVER SEEN A HOUSE LIKE THAT BEFORE!
A VERY MERRY UNBIRTH-DAY!
TO ME?
TO YOU!
A VERY MERRY UN-BIRTHDAY!
THE... THE KETTLES AND THE TEAPOTS...
... ARE DANCING ON THEIR OWN!

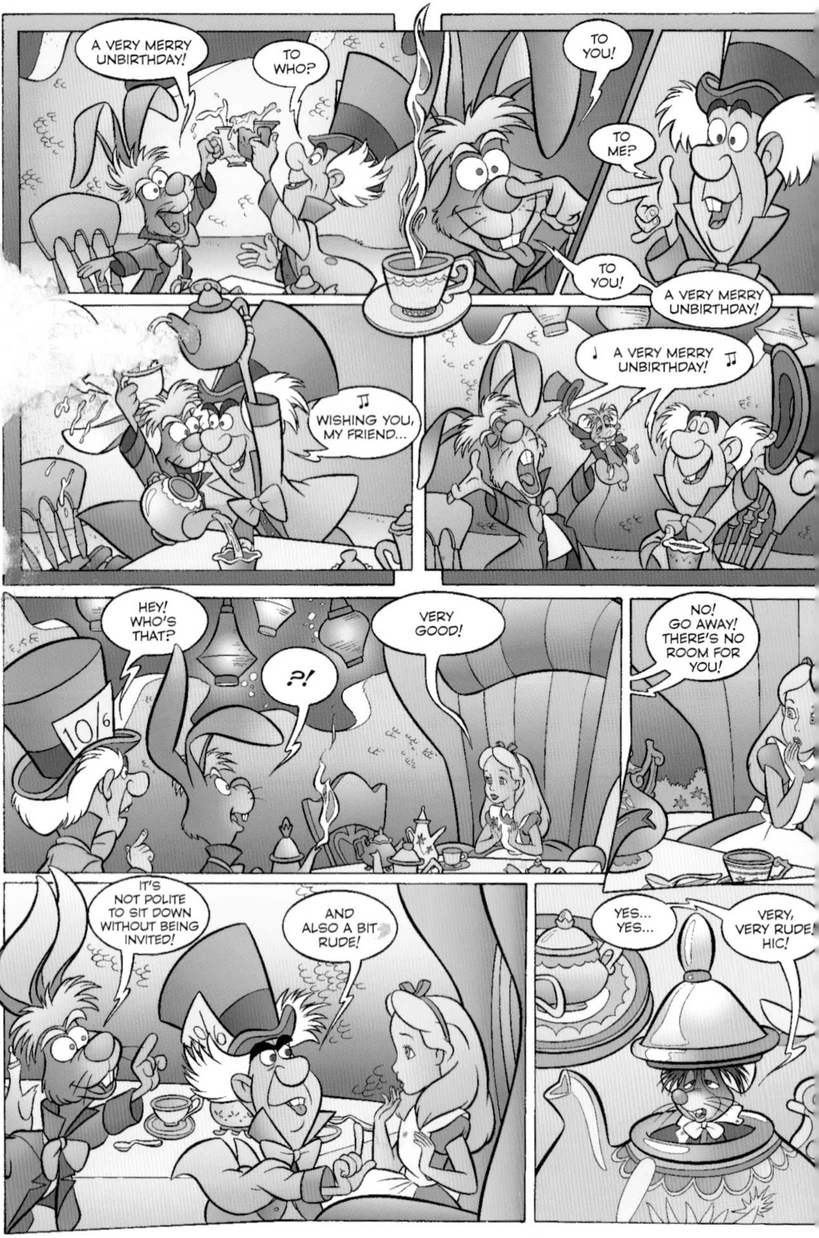
A VERY MERRY UNBIRTHDAY!
TO WHO?
TO YOU!
TO ME?
TO YOU!
A VERY MERRY UNBIRTHDAY!
WISHING YOU, MY FRIEND...
A VERY MERRY UNBIRTHDAY!
HEY! WHO'S THAT?
?!
VERY GOOD!
NO! GO AWAY! THERE'S NO ROOM FOR YOU!
IT'S NOT POLITE TO SIT DOWN WITHOUT BEING INVITED!
AND ALSO A BIT RUDE!
YES... YES...
VERY, VERY RUDE! HIC!

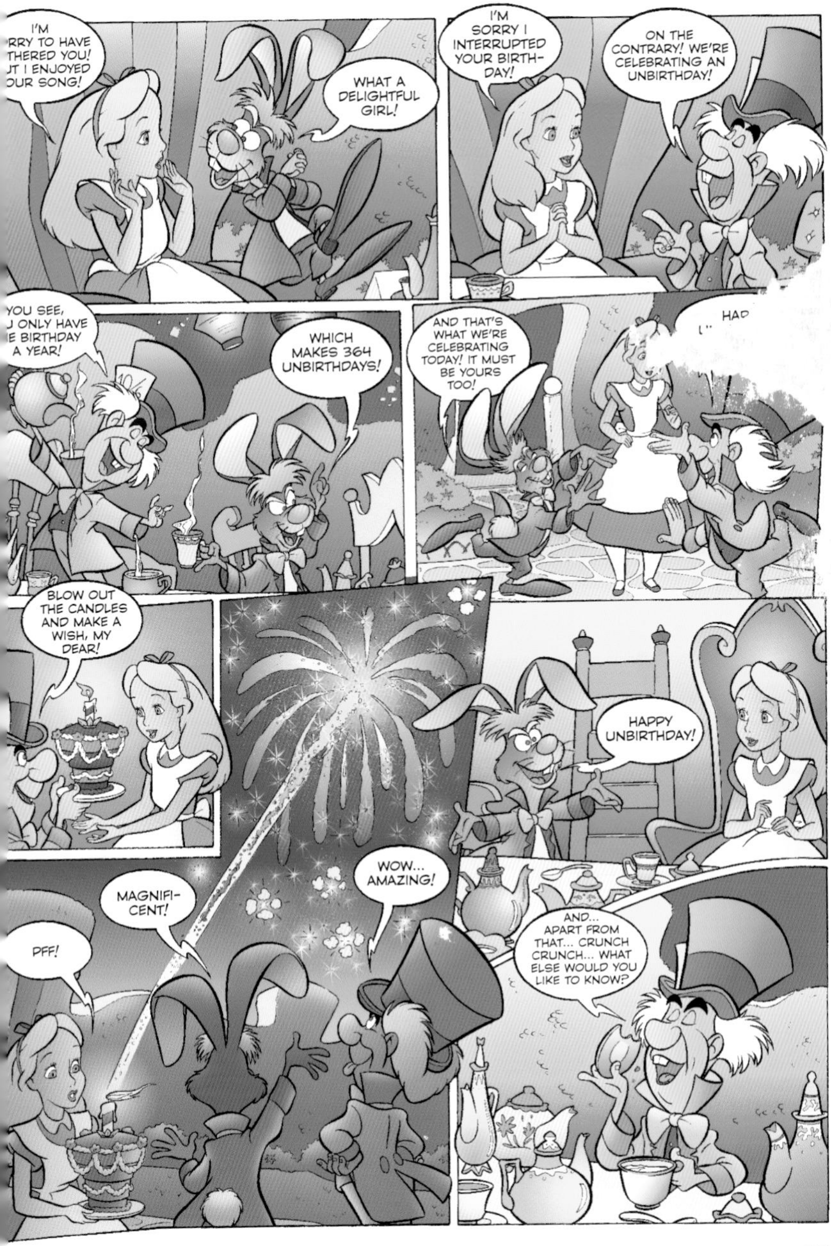
I'M
RRY TO HAVE
THERED YOU!
JT I ENJOYED
OUR SONG!
WHAT A DELIGHTFUL GIRL!
I'M SORRY I INTERRUPTED YOUR BIRTH-DAY!
ON THE CONTRARY! WE'RE CELEBRATING AN UNBIRTHDAY!
YOU SEE,
J ONLY HAVE
E BIRTHDAY
A YEAR!
WHICH MAKES 364 UNBIRTHDAYS!
AND THAT'S WHAT WE'RE CELEBRATING TODAY! IT MUST BE YOURS TOO!
BLOW OUT THE CANDLES AND MAKE A WISH, MY DEAR!
HAPPY UNBIRTHDAY!
MAGNIFI-CENT!
WOW... AMAZING!
PFF!
AND... APART FROM THAT... CRUNCH CRUNCH... WHAT ELSE WOULD YOU LIKE TO KNOW?

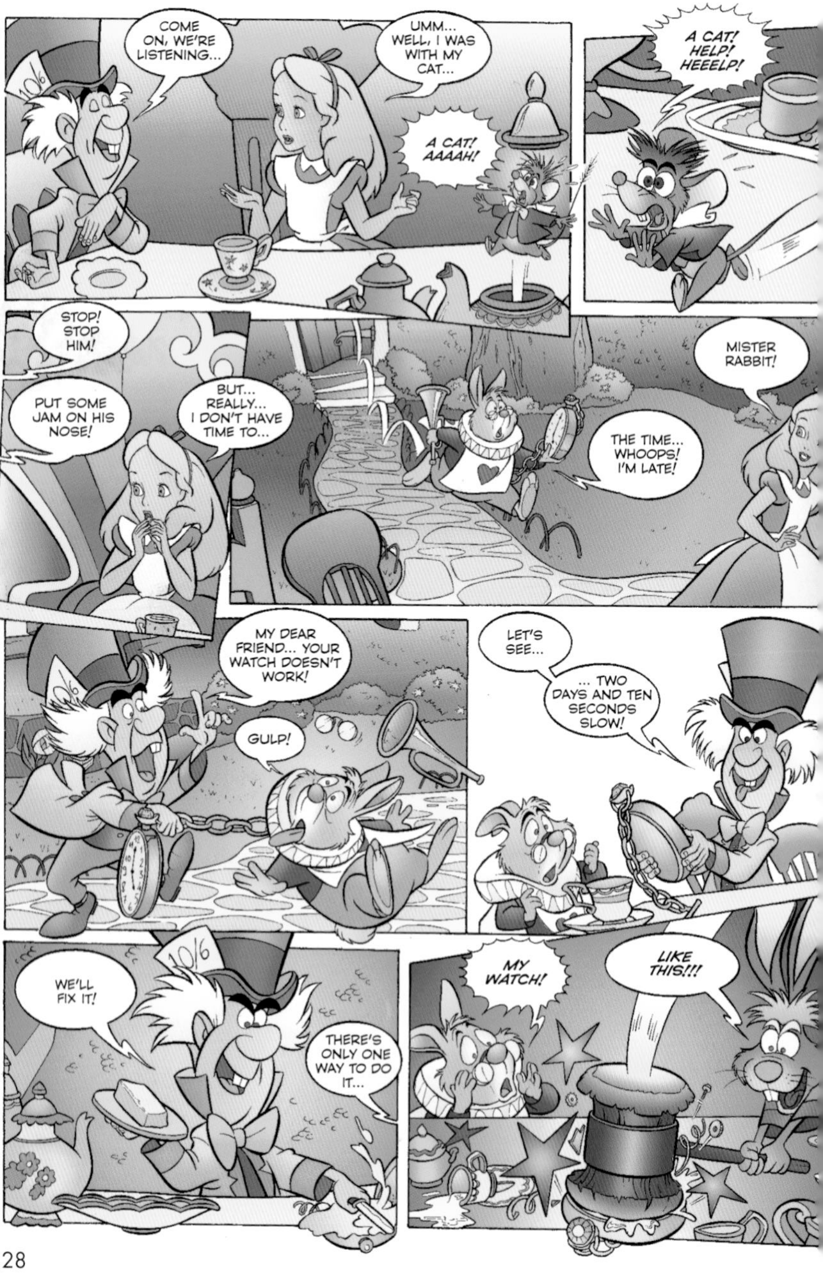
COME ON, WE'RE LISTENING...
UMM... WELL, I WAS WITH MY CAT...
A CAT! AAAAH!
A CAT! HELP! HEEELP!
STOP! STOP HIM!
PUT SOME JAM ON HIS NOSE!
BUT... REALLY... I DON'T HAVE TIME TO...
MISTER RABBIT!
THE TIME... WHOOPS! I'M LATE!
MY DEAR FRIEND... YOUR WATCH DOESN'T WORK!
GULP!
LET'S SEE...
... TWO DAYS AND TEN SECONDS SLOW!
WE'LL FIX IT!
THERE'S ONLY ONE WAY TO DO IT...
MY WATCH!
LIKE THIS!!!

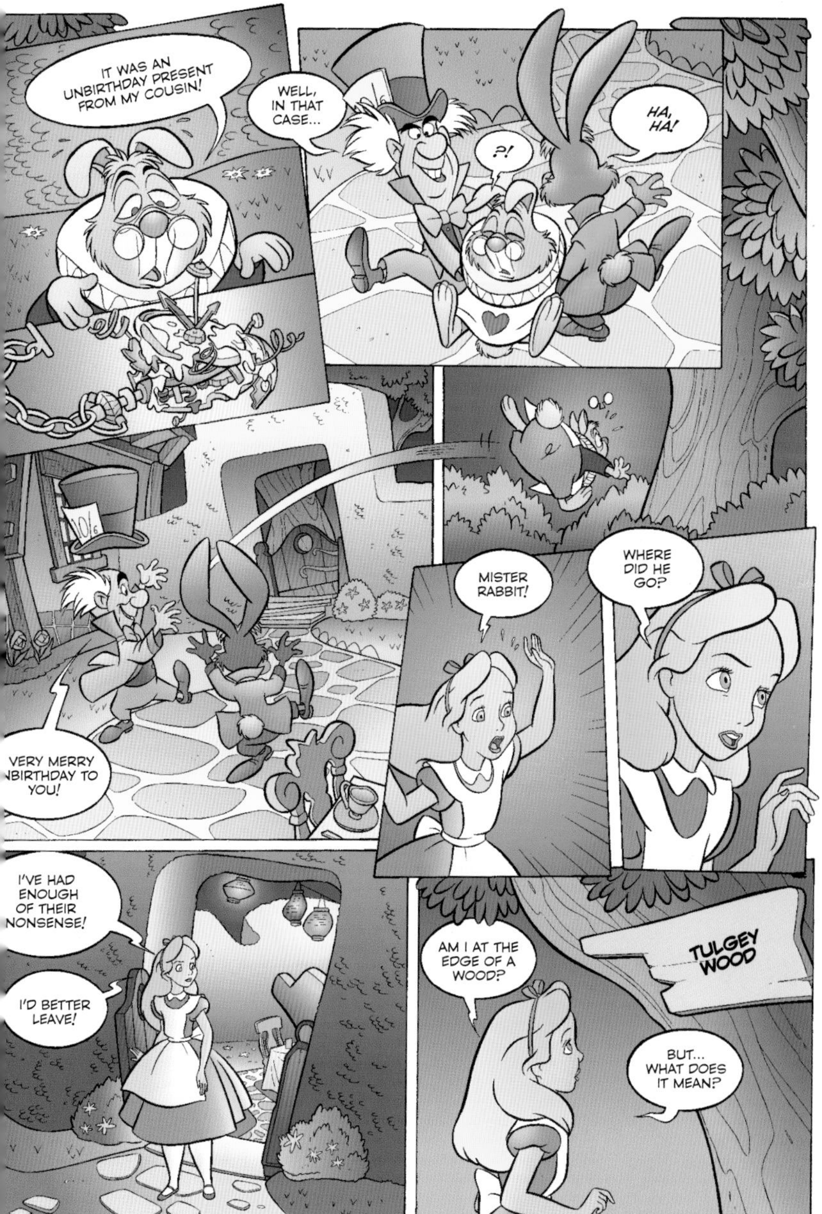
IT WAS AN UNBIRTHDAY PRESENT FROM MY COUSIN!
WELL, IN THAT CASE...
?!
HA, HA!
10/6
VERY MERRY NBIRTHDAY TO YOU!
MISTER RABBIT!
WHERE DID HE GO?
I'VE HAD ENOUGH OF THEIR NONSENSE!
I'D BETTER LEAVE!
AM I AT THE EDGE OF A WOOD?
TULGEY WOOD
BUT... WHAT DOES IT MEAN?

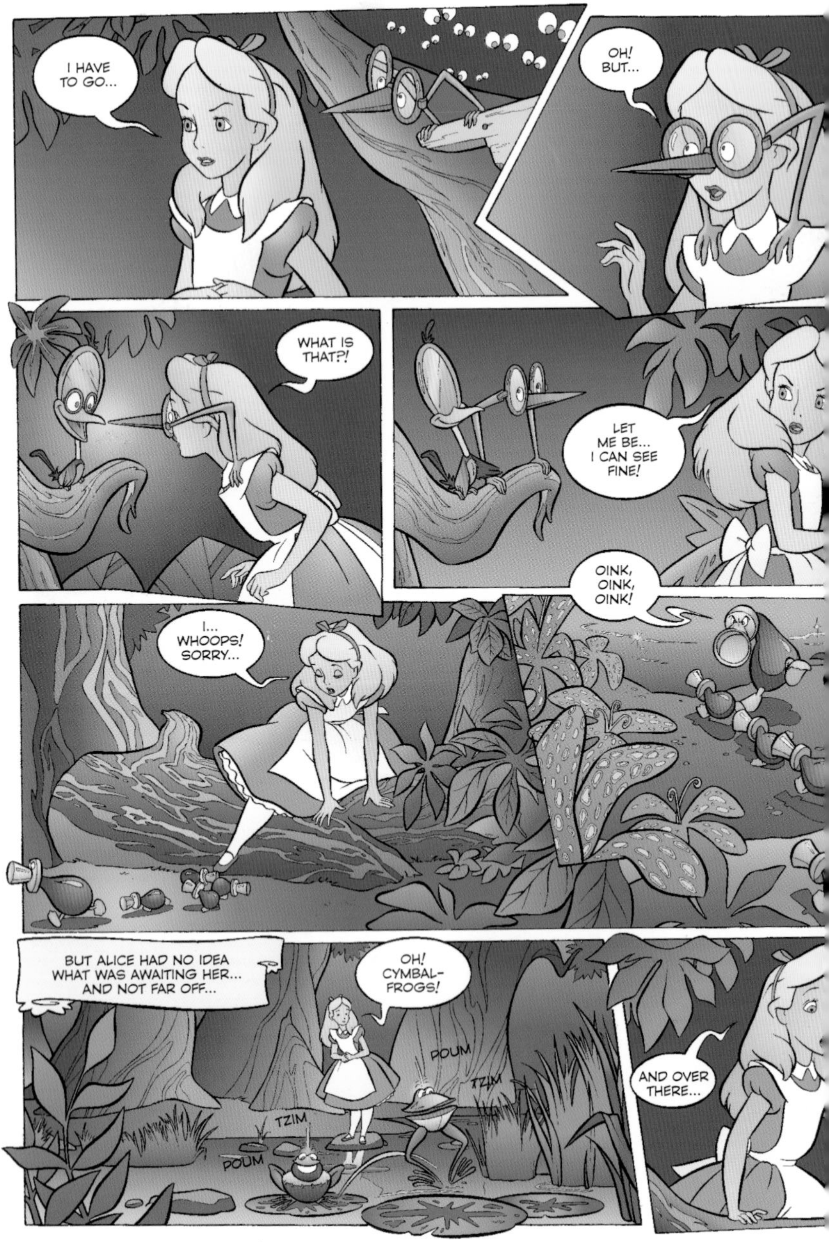
I HAVE TO GO...
OH! BUT...
WHAT IS THAT?!
LET ME BE... I CAN SEE FINE!
I... WHOOPS! SORRY...
OINK, OINK, OINK!
BUT ALICE HAD NO IDEA WHAT WAS AWAITING HER... AND NOT FAR OFF...
OH! CYMBAL-FROGS!
POUM
TZIM
TZIM
POUM
AND OVER THERE...

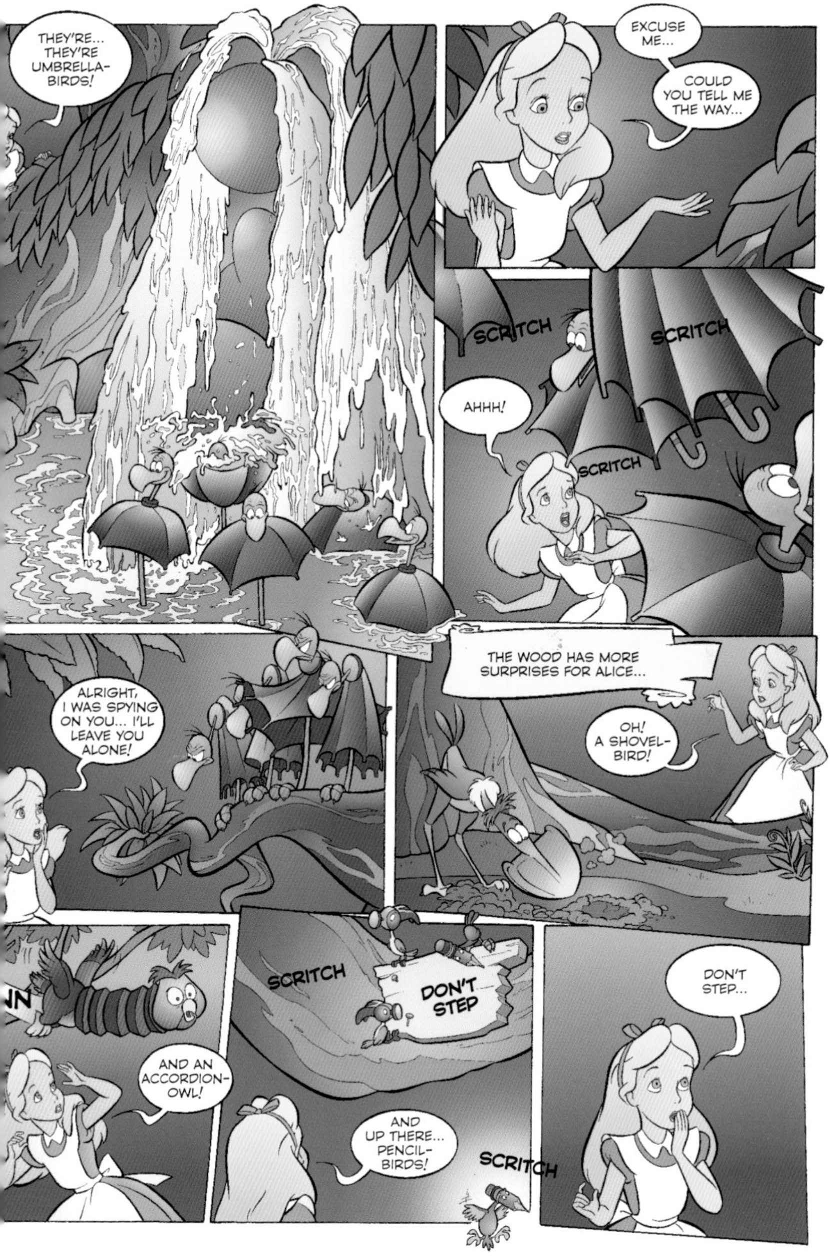
THEY'RE... THEY'RE UMBRELLA-BIRDS!
EXCUSE ME...
COULD YOU TELL ME THE WAY...
SCRITCH
SCRITCH
AHHH!
SCRITCH
ALRIGHT, I WAS SPYING ON YOU... I'LL LEAVE YOU ALONE!
THE WOOD HAS MORE SURPRISES FOR ALICE...
OH! A SHOVEL-BIRD!
AND AN ACCORDION-OWL!
SCRITCH
DON'T STEP
AND UP THERE... PENCIL-BIRDS!
SCRITCH
DON'T STEP...

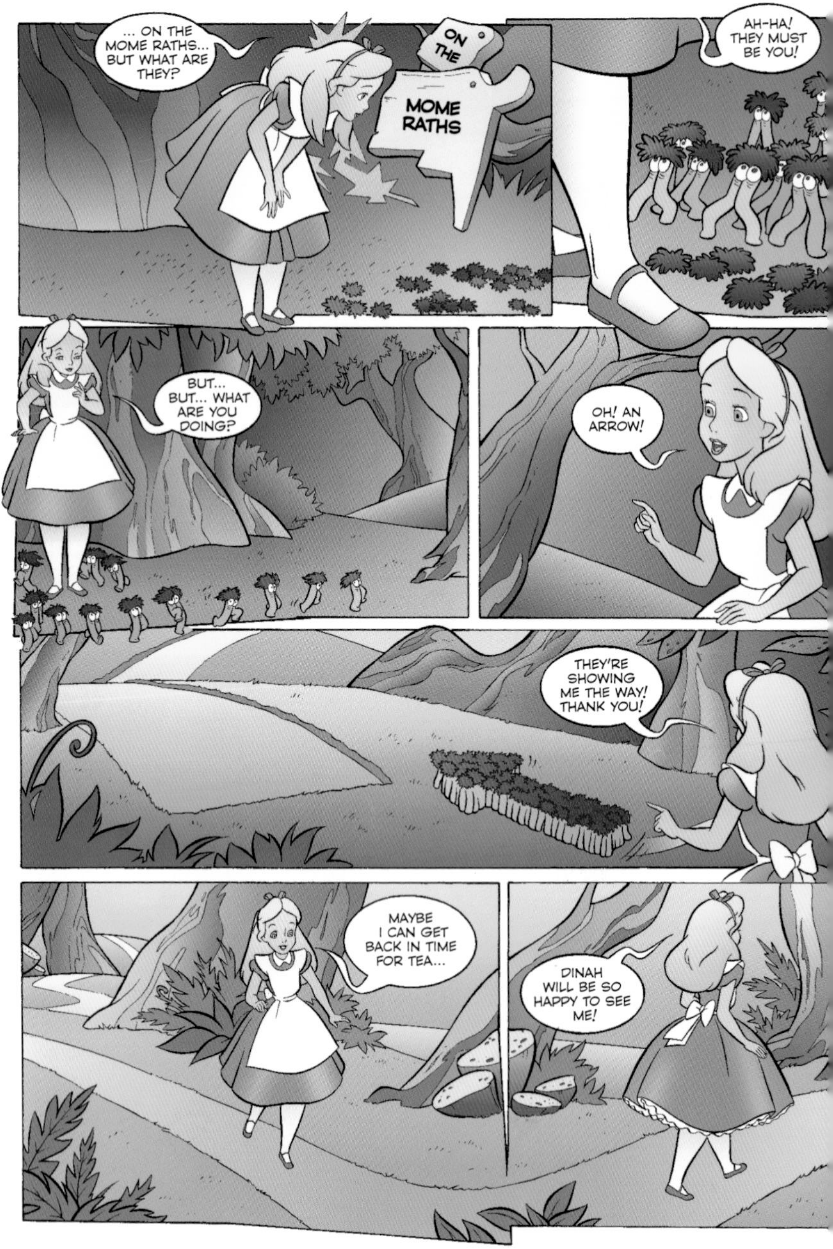
... ON THE MOME RATHS... BUT WHAT ARE THEY?
ON THE
MOME RATHS
AH-HA! THEY MUST BE YOU!
BUT... BUT... WHAT ARE YOU DOING?
OH! AN ARROW!
THEY'RE SHOWING ME THE WAY! THANK YOU!
MAYBE I CAN GET BACK IN TIME FOR TEA...
DINAH WILL BE SO HAPPY TO SEE ME!

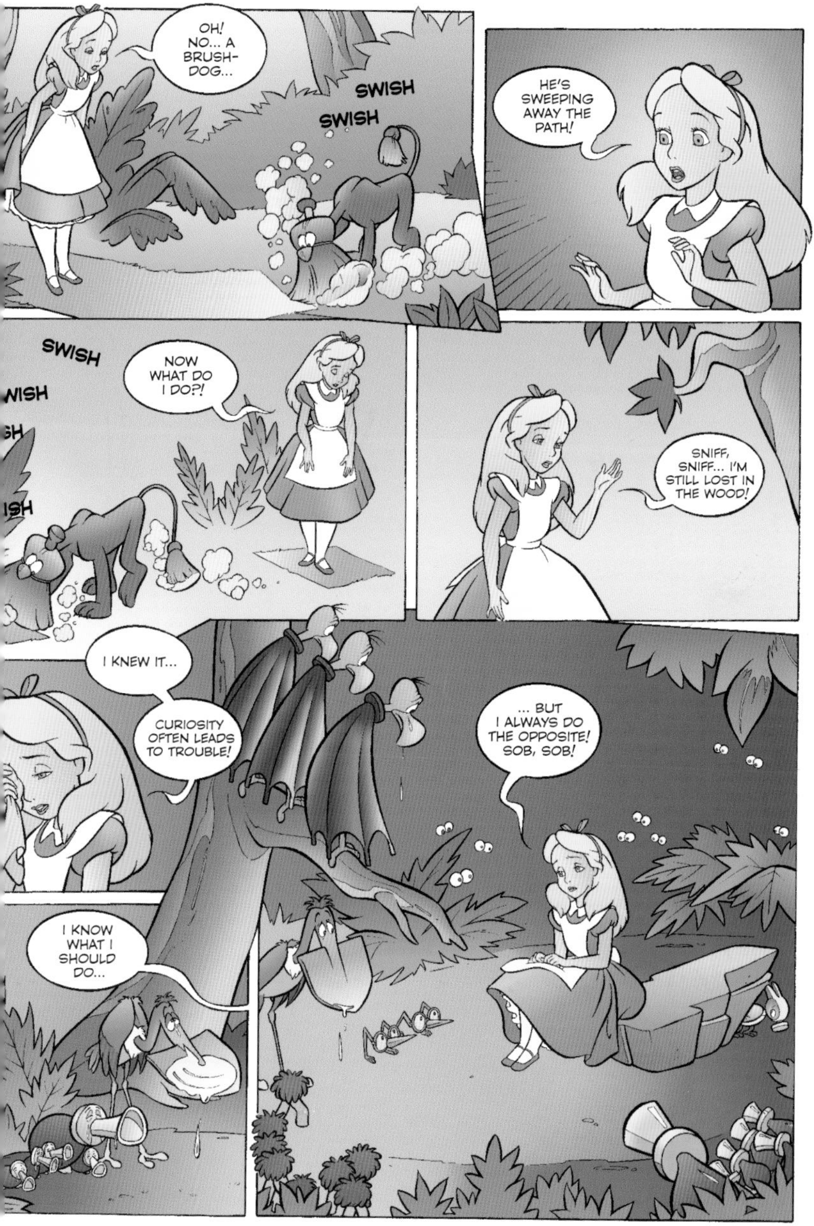

OH! NO... A BRUSH-DOG...
SWISH
SWISH
HE'S SWEEPING AWAY THE PATH!
SWISH
NOW WHAT DO I DO?!
SNIFF, SNIFF... I'M STILL LOST IN THE WOOD!
I KNEW IT...
CURIOSITY OFTEN LEADS TO TROUBLE!
I KNOW WHAT I SHOULD DO...
... BUT I ALWAYS DO THE OPPOSITE! SOB, SOB!

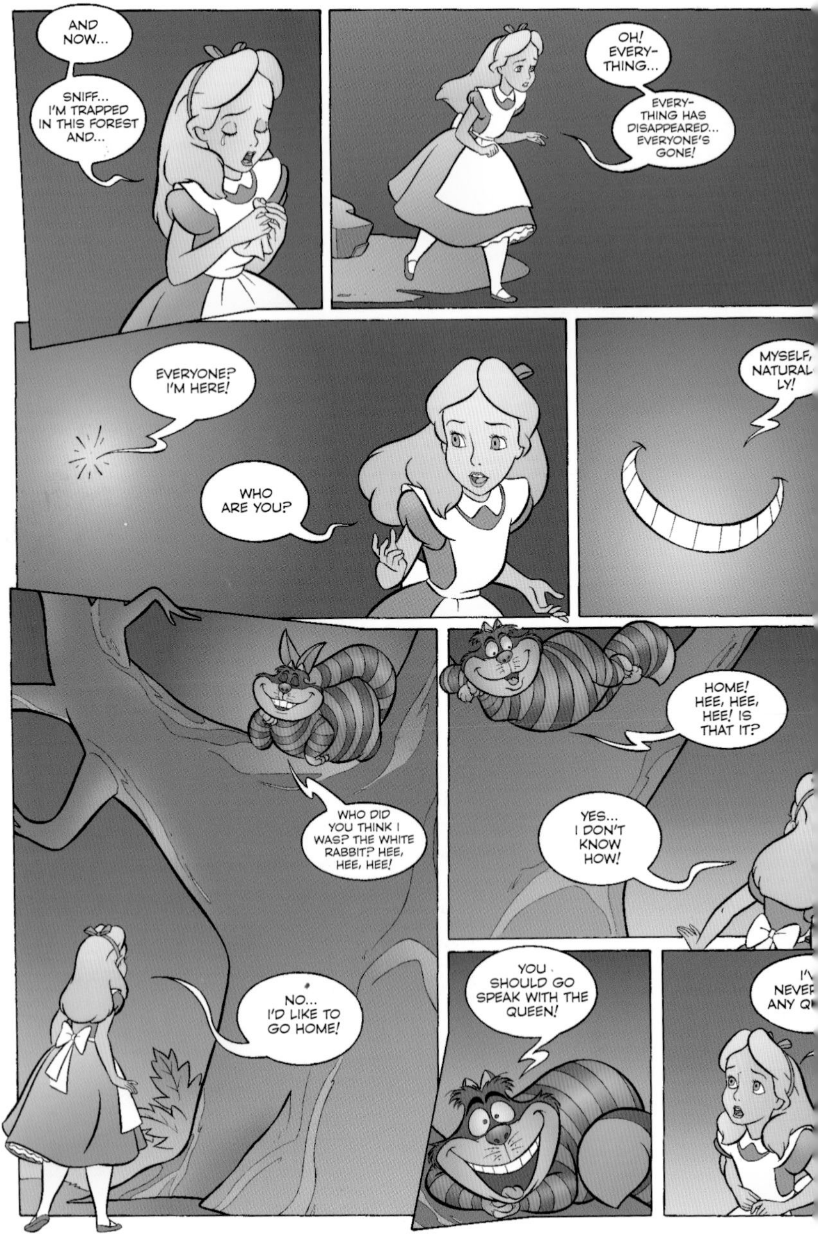

AND NOW...
SNIFF... I'M TRAPPED IN THIS FOREST AND...
OH! EVERY-THING...
EVERY-THING HAS DISAPPEARED... EVERYONE'S GONE!
EVERYONE? I'M HERE!
WHO ARE YOU?
MYSELF, NATURAL-LY!
WHO DID YOU THINK I WAS? THE WHITE RABBIT? HEE, HEE, HEE!
NO... I'D LIKE TO GO HOME!
HOME! HEE, HEE, HEE! IS THAT IT?
YES... I DON'T KNOW HOW!
YOU SHOULD GO SPEAK WITH THE QUEEN!

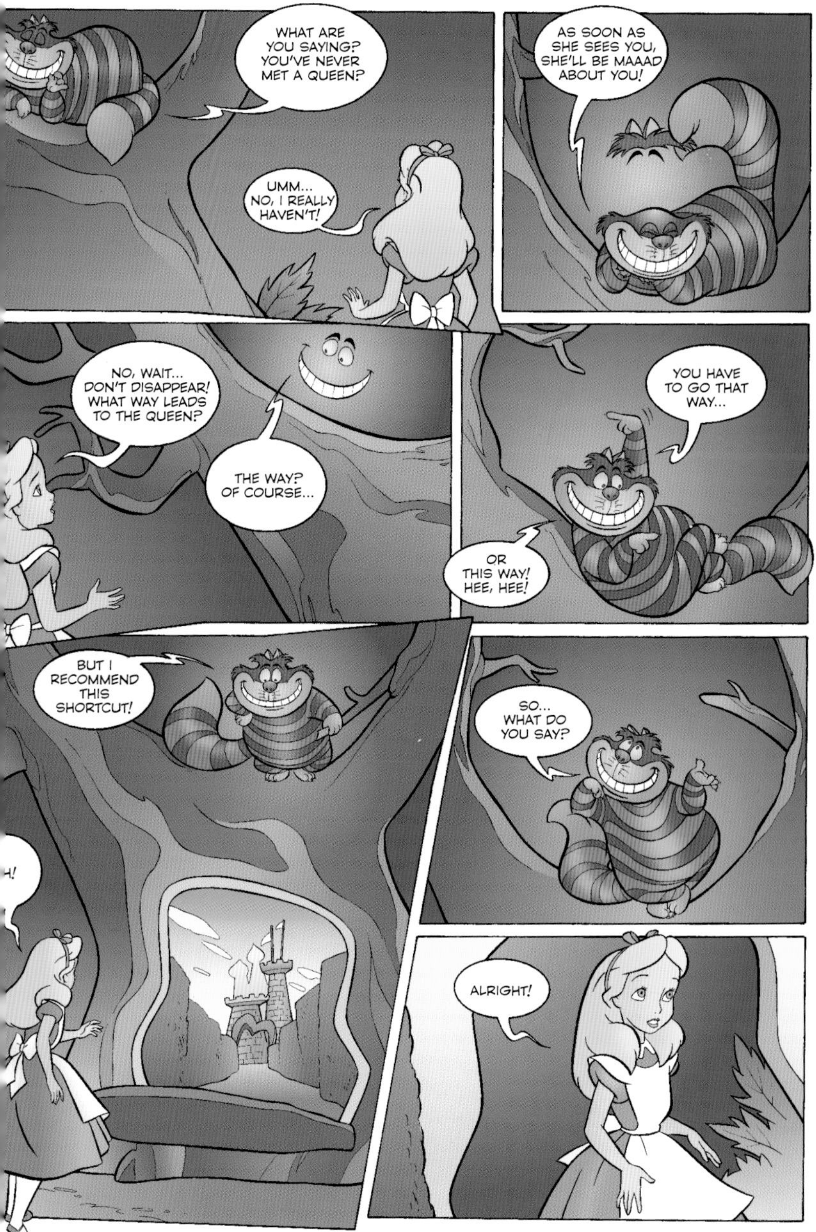
WHAT ARE YOU SAYING? YOU'VE NEVER MET A QUEEN?
UMM... NO, I REALLY HAVEN'T!
AS SOON AS SHE SEES YOU, SHE'LL BE MAAAD ABOUT YOU!
NO, WAIT... DON'T DISAPPEAR! WHAT WAY LEADS TO THE QUEEN?
THE WAY? OF COURSE...
YOU HAVE TO GO THAT WAY...
OR THIS WAY! HEE, HEE!
BUT I RECOMMEND THIS SHORTCUT!
SO... WHAT DO YOU SAY?
ALRIGHT!

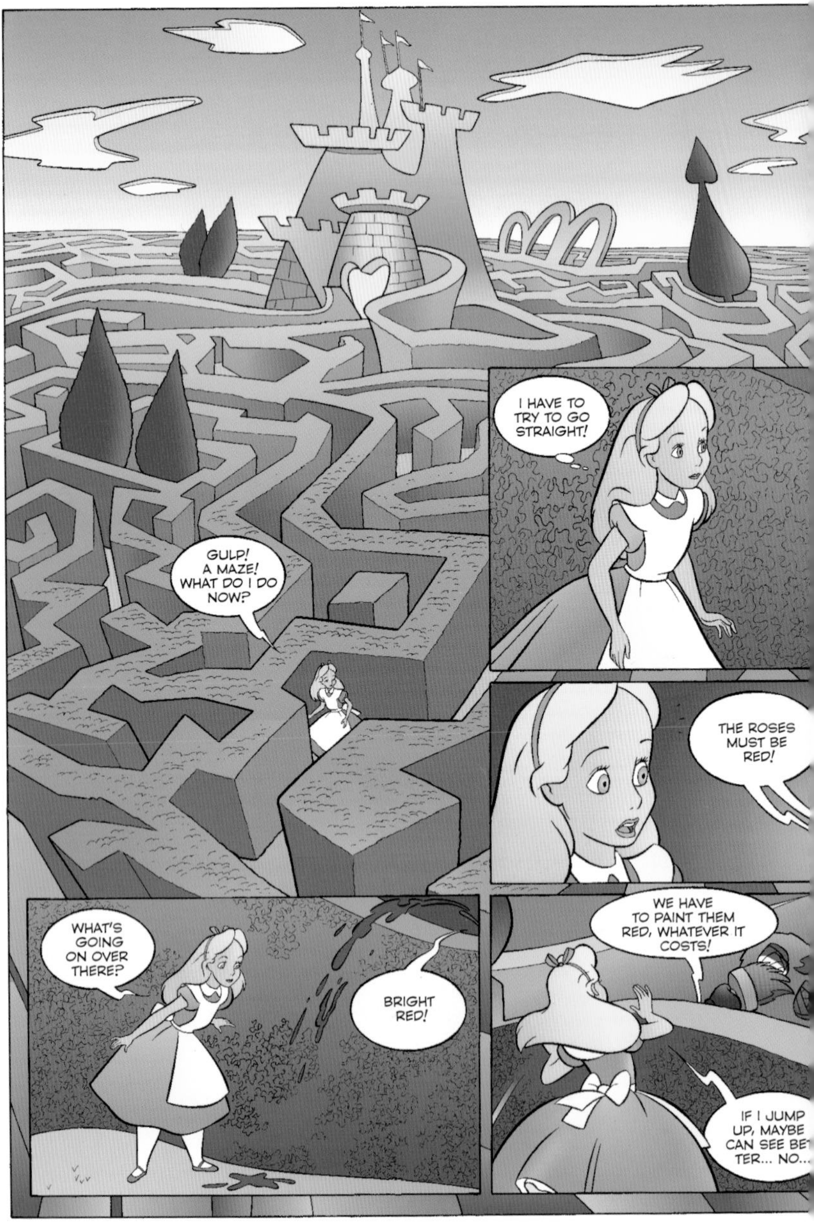
GULP! A MAZE! WHAT DO I DO NOW?
I HAVE TO TRY TO GO STRAIGHT!
THE ROSES MUST BE RED!
WHAT'S GOING ON OVER THERE?
BRIGHT RED!
WE HAVE TO PAINT THEM RED, WHATEVER IT COSTS!
IF I JUMP UP, MAYBE CAN SEE BET TER... NO...

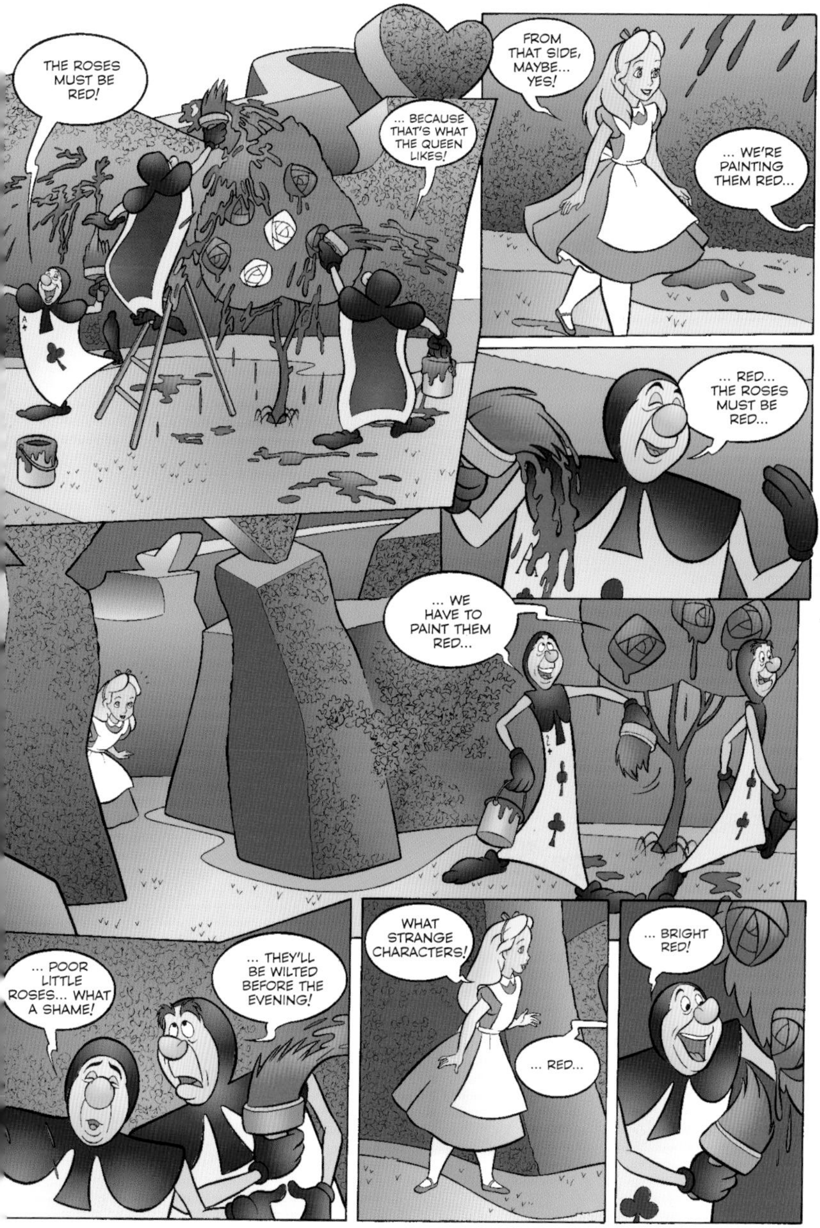
THE ROSES MUST BE RED!
... BECAUSE THAT'S WHAT THE QUEEN LIKES!
FROM THAT SIDE, MAYBE... YES!
... WE'RE PAINTING THEM RED...
... RED... THE ROSES MUST BE RED...
... WE HAVE TO PAINT THEM RED...
... POOR LITTLE ROSES... WHAT A SHAME!
... THEY'LL BE WILTED BEFORE THE EVENING!
WHAT STRANGE CHARACTERS!
... RED...
... BRIGHT RED!

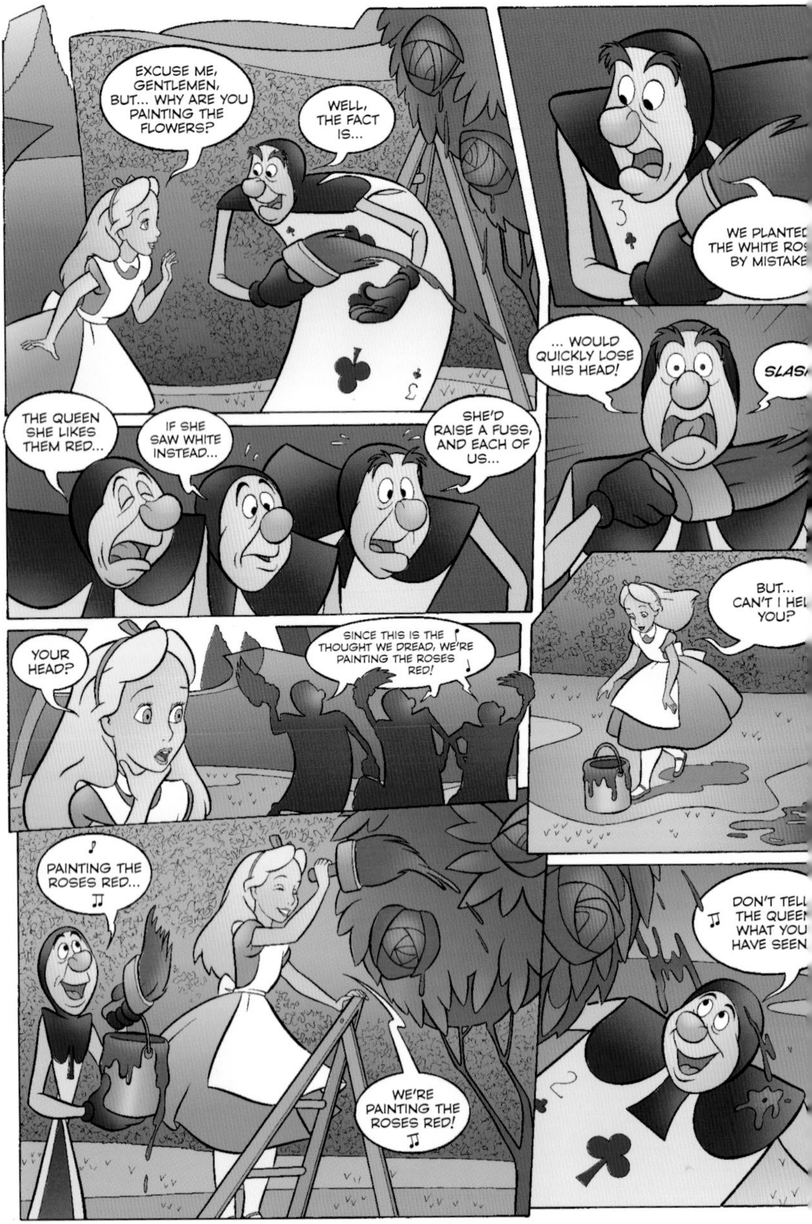
EXCUSE ME, GENTLEMEN, BUT... WHY ARE YOU PAINTING THE FLOWERS?
WELL, THE FACT IS...
WE PLANTED THE WHITE RO BY MISTAKE
THE QUEEN SHE LIKES THEM RED...
IF SHE SAW WHITE INSTEAD...
SHE'D RAISE A FUSS, AND EACH OF US...
... WOULD QUICKLY LOSE HIS HEAD!
SLAS
YOUR HEAD?
SINCE THIS IS THE THOUGHT WE DREAD, WE'RE PAINTING THE ROSES RED!
BUT... CAN'T I HE YOU?
PAINTING THE ROSES RED...
WE'RE PAINTING THE ROSES RED!
DON'T TEL THE QUEE WHAT YOU HAVE SEEN

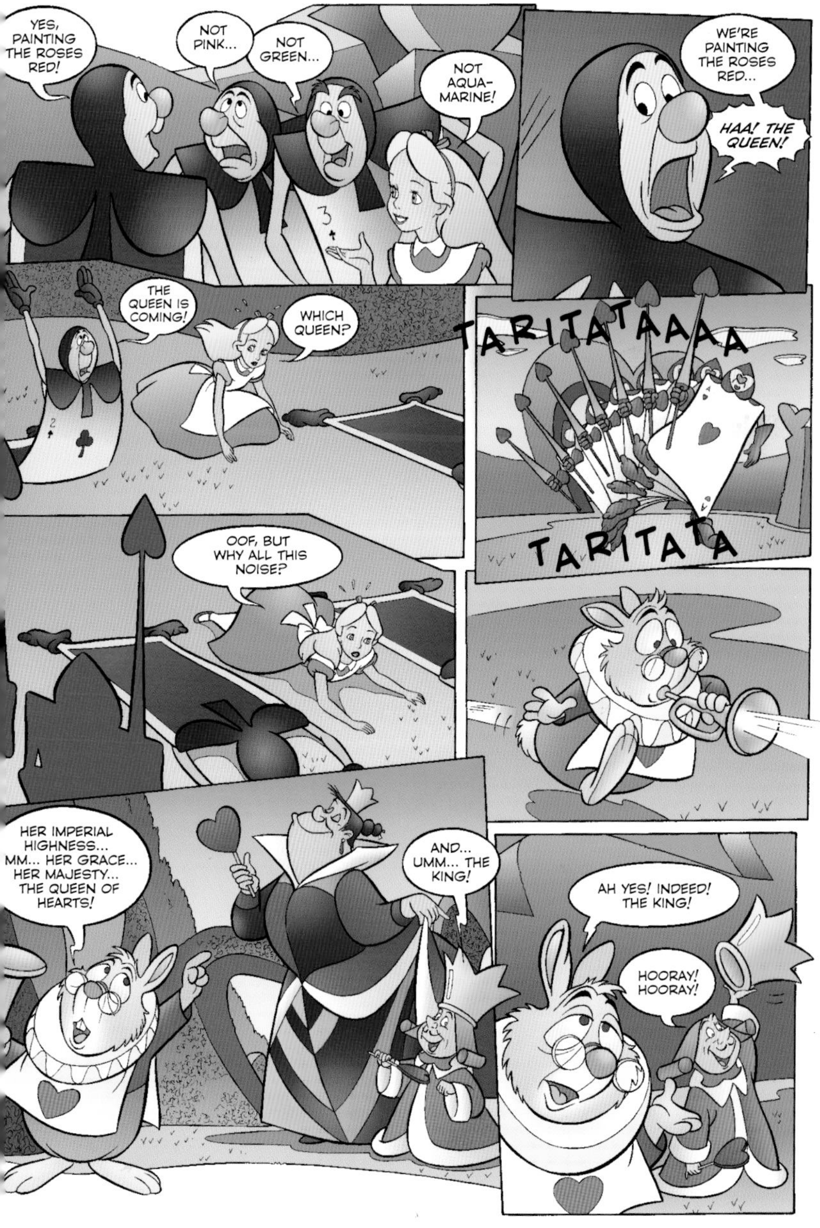
YES, PAINTING THE ROSES RED!
NOT PINK...
NOT GREEN...
NOT AQUA-MARINE!
WE'RE PAINTING THE ROSES RED...
HAA! THE QUEEN!
THE QUEEN IS COMING!
WHICH QUEEN?
TARITATAAAA
OOF, BUT WHY ALL THIS NOISE?
TARITATA
HER IMPERIAL HIGHNESS... MM... HER GRACE... HER MAJESTY... THE QUEEN OF HEARTS!
AND... UMM... THE KING!
AH YES! INDEED! THE KING!
HOORAY! HOORAY!

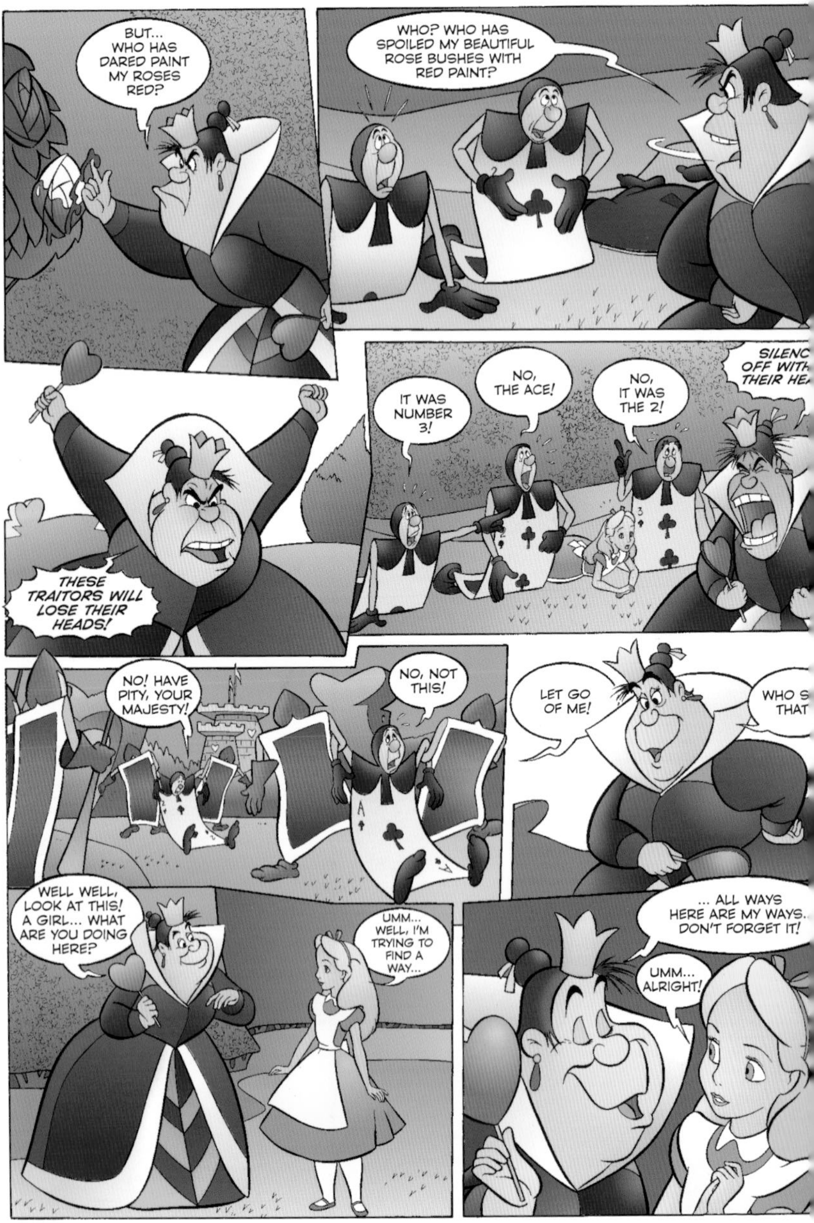
BUT... WHO HAS DARED PAINT MY ROSES RED?
WHO? WHO HAS SPOILED MY BEAUTIFUL ROSE BUSHES WITH RED PAINT?
THESE TRAITORS WILL LOSE THEIR HEADS!
IT WAS NUMBER 3!
NO, THE ACE!
NO, IT WAS THE 2!
SILENC
OFF WITH
THEIR HE
NO! HAVE PITY, YOUR MAJESTY!
NO, NOT THIS!
LET GO OF ME!
WHO S
THAT
WELL WELL, LOOK AT THIS! A GIRL... WHAT ARE YOU DOING HERE?
UMM... WELL, I'M TRYING TO FIND A WAY...
... ALL WAYS HERE ARE MY WAYS... DON'T FORGET IT!
UMM... ALRIGHT!

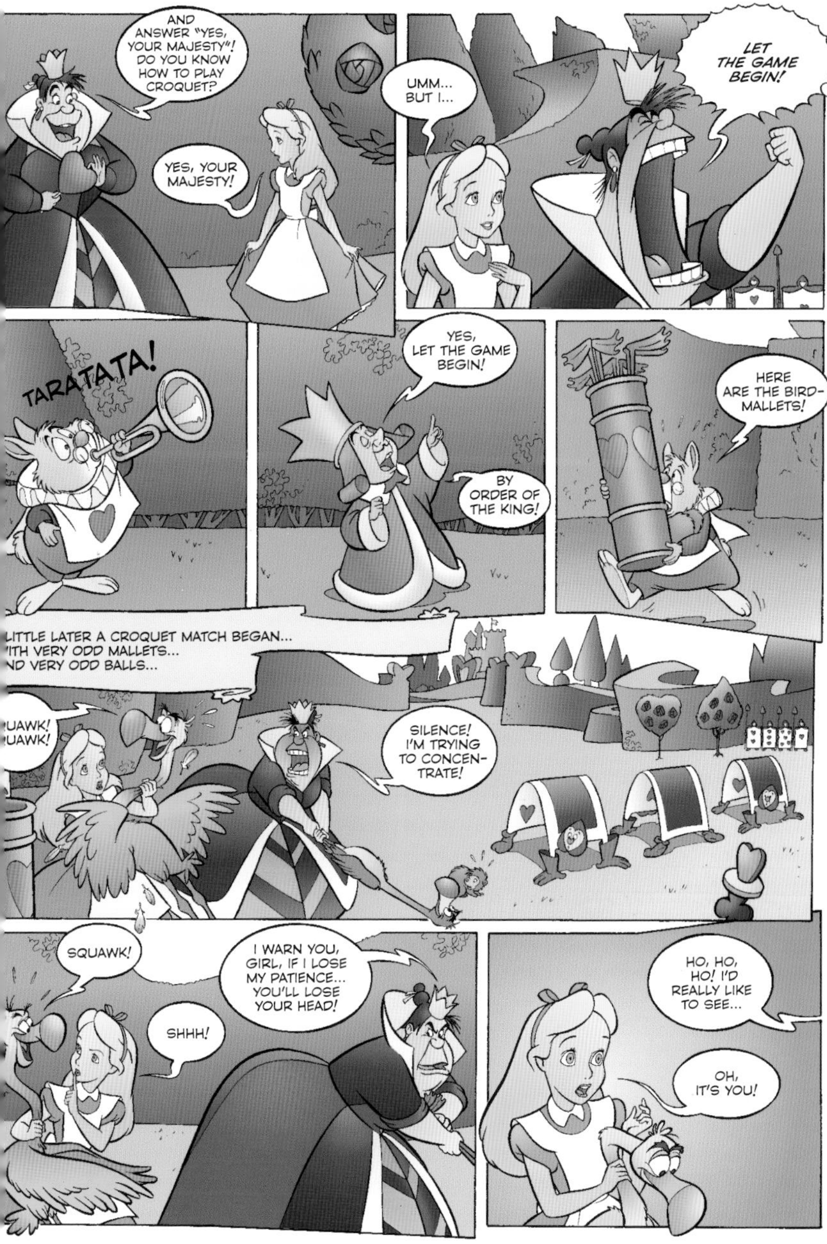

AND ANSWER "YES, YOUR MAJESTY"! DO YOU KNOW HOW TO PLAY CROQUET?
YES, YOUR MAJESTY!
UMM... BUT I...
LET THE GAME BEGIN!
TARATATA!
YES, LET THE GAME BEGIN!
BY ORDER OF THE KING!
HERE ARE THE BIRD-MALLETS!
LITTLE LATER A CROQUET MATCH BEGAN... ITH VERY ODD MALLETS... ND VERY ODD BALLS...
UAWK! UAWK!
SILENCE! I'M TRYING TO CONCEN-TRATE!
SQUAWK!
I WARN YOU, GIRL, IF I LOSE MY PATIENCE... YOU'LL LOSE YOUR HEAD!
SHHH!
HO, HO, HO! I'D REALLY LIKE TO SEE...
OH, IT'S YOU!

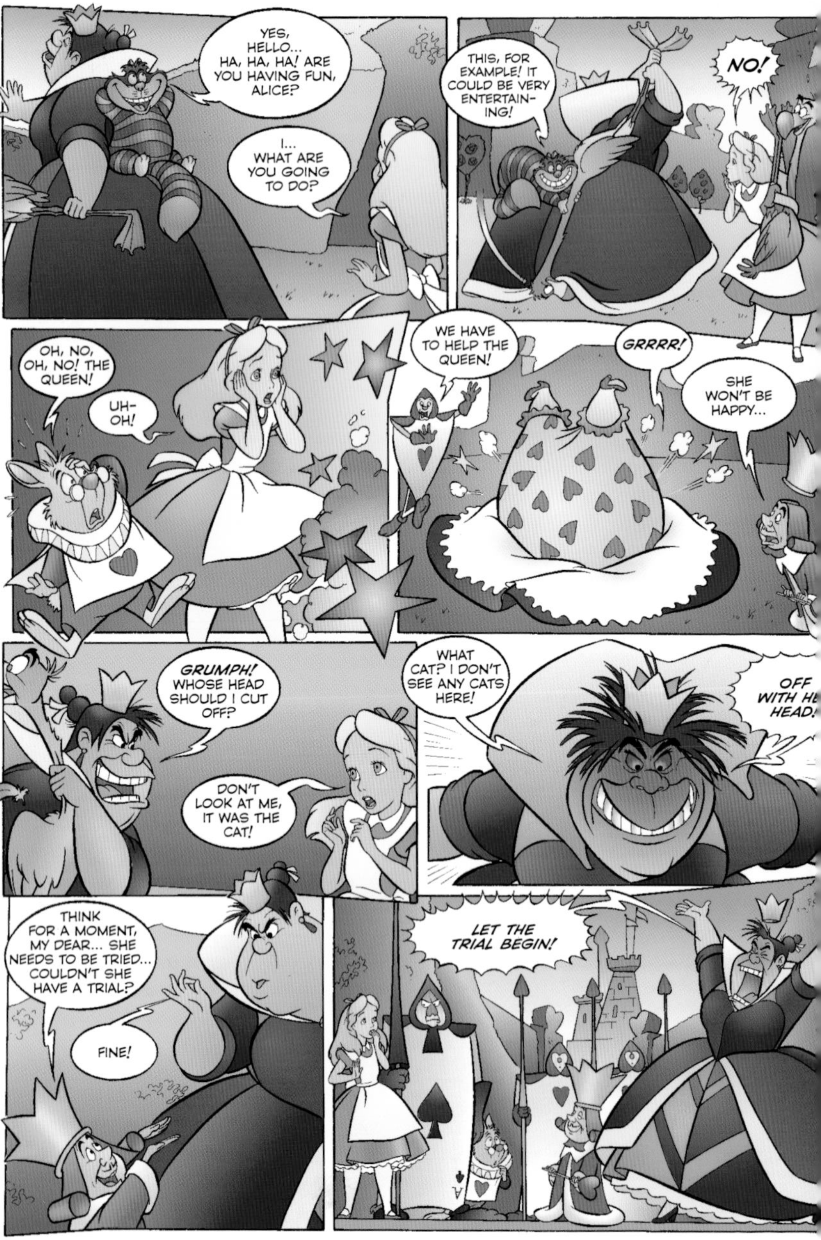
YES, HELLO... HA, HA, HA! ARE YOU HAVING FUN, ALICE?
I... WHAT ARE YOU GOING TO DO?
THIS, FOR EXAMPLE! IT COULD BE VERY ENTERTAIN-ING!
NO!
OH, NO, OH, NO! THE QUEEN!
UH-OH!
WE HAVE TO HELP THE QUEEN!
GRRRR!
SHE WON'T BE HAPPY...
GRUMPH! WHOSE HEAD SHOULD I CUT OFF?
DON'T LOOK AT ME, IT WAS THE CAT!
WHAT CAT? I DON'T SEE ANY CATS HERE!
THINK FOR A MOMENT, MY DEAR... SHE NEEDS TO BE TRIED... COULDN'T SHE HAVE A TRIAL?
FINE!
LET THE TRIAL BEGIN!

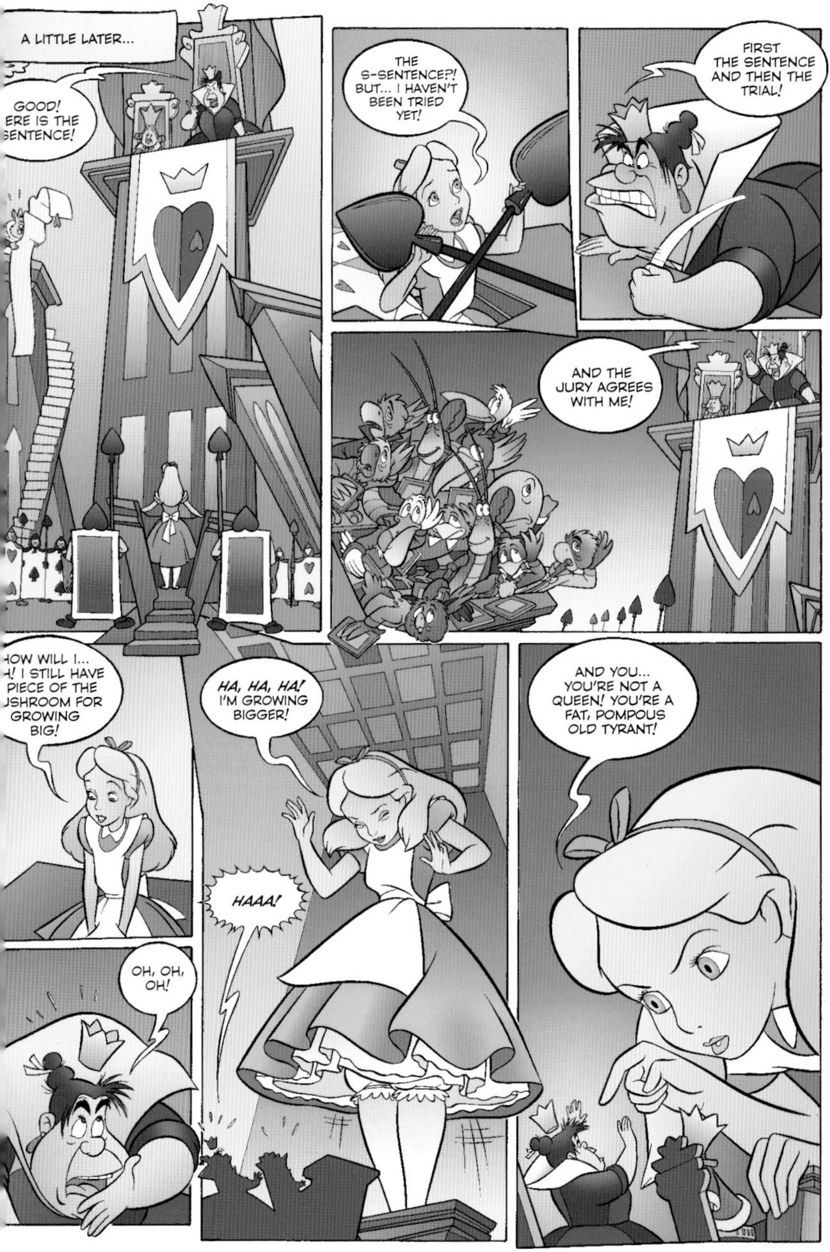
A LITTLE LATER...
GOOD! ERE IS THE SENTENCE!
THE S-SENTENCE?! BUT... I HAVEN'T BEEN TRIED YET!
FIRST THE SENTENCE AND THEN THE TRIAL!
AND THE JURY AGREES WITH ME!
HOW WILL I... H! I STILL HAVE PIECE OF THE USHROOM FOR GROWING BIG!
OH, OH, OH!
HA, HA, HA! I'M GROWING BIGGER!
HAAA!
AND YOU... YOU'RE NOT A QUEEN! YOU'RE A FAT, POMPOUS OLD TYRANT!

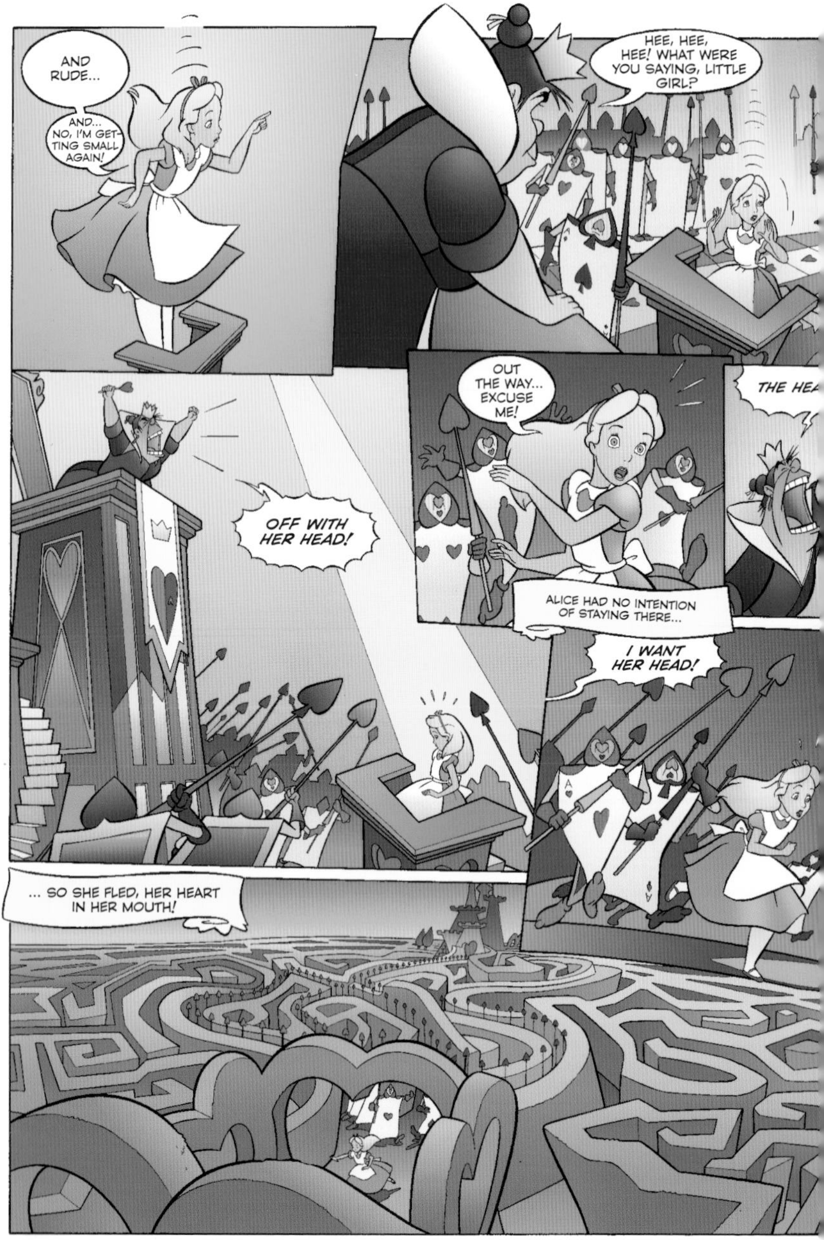
AND RUDE...
AND... NO, I'M GETTING SMALL AGAIN!
HEE, HEE, HEE! WHAT WERE YOU SAYING, LITTLE GIRL?
OFF WITH HER HEAD!
OUT THE WAY... EXCUSE ME!
ALICE HAD NO INTENTION OF STAYING THERE...
I WANT HER HEAD!
... SO SHE FLED, HER HEART IN HER MOUTH!

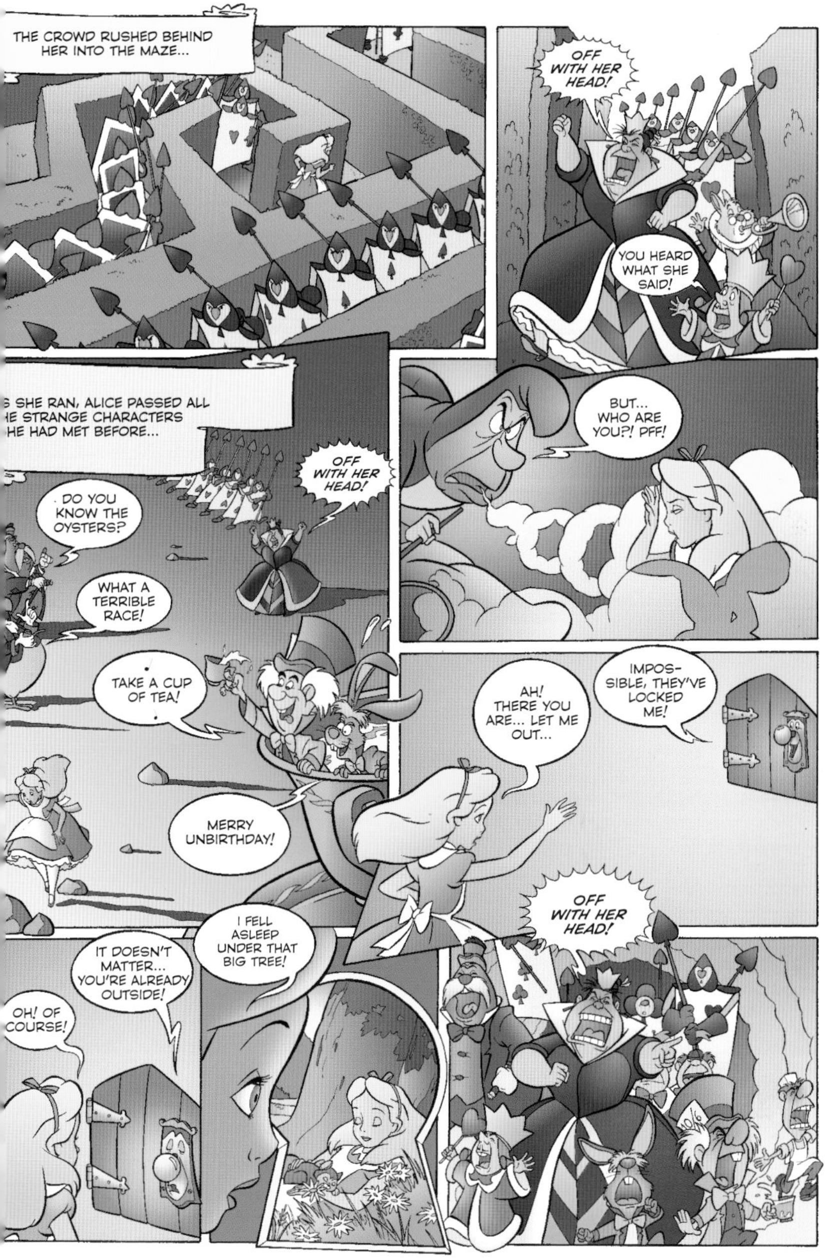
THE CROWD RUSHED BEHIND HER INTO THE MAZE...
OFF WITH HER HEAD!
YOU HEARD WHAT SHE SAID!
S SHE RAN, ALICE PASSED ALL HE STRANGE CHARACTERS HE HAD MET BEFORE...
OFF WITH HER HEAD!
DO YOU KNOW THE OYSTERS?
WHAT A TERRIBLE RACE!
TAKE A CUP OF TEA!
MERRY UNBIRTHDAY!
BUT... WHO ARE YOU?! PFF!
IMPOS-SIBLE, THEY'VE LOCKED ME!
AH! THERE YOU ARE... LET ME OUT...
I FELL ASLEEP UNDER THAT BIG TREE!
IT DOESN'T MATTER... YOU'RE ALREADY OUTSIDE!
OH! OF COURSE!
OFF WITH HER HEAD!

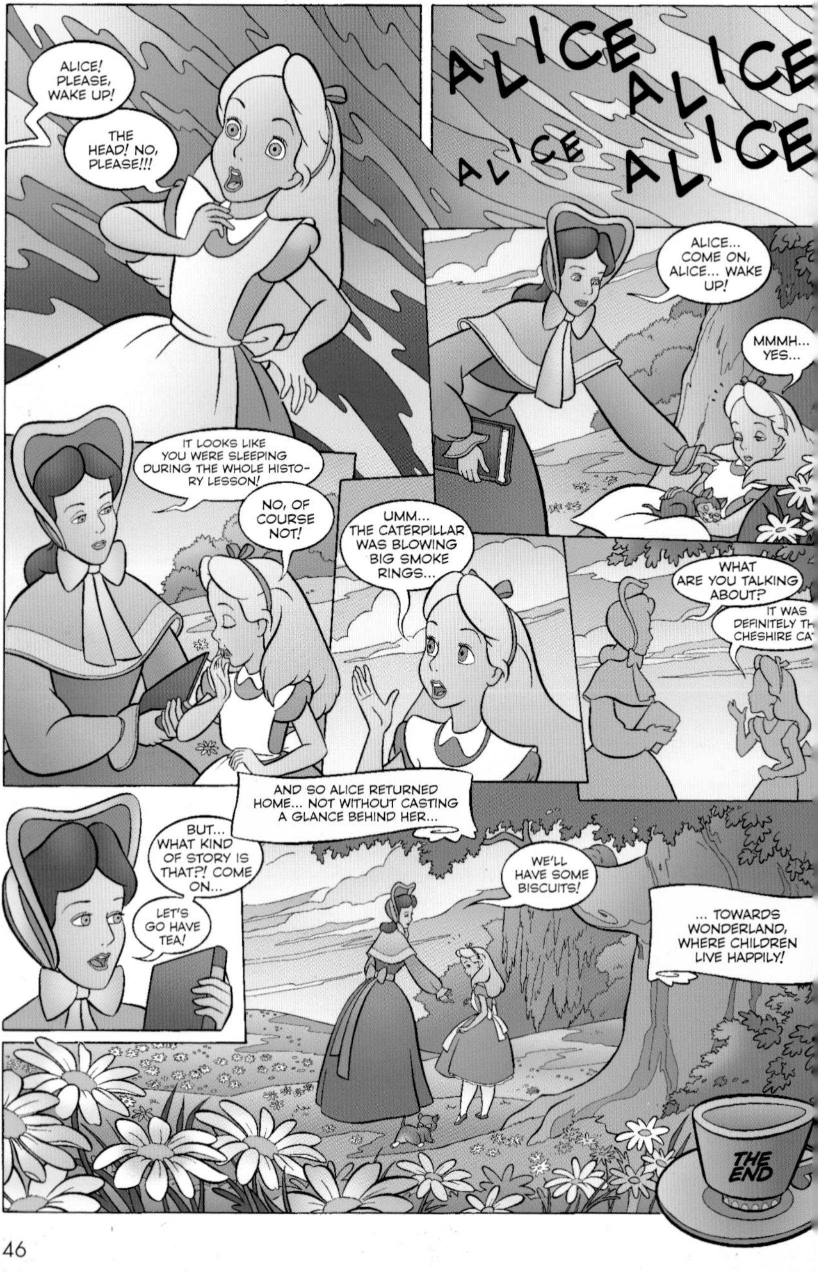
ALICE! PLEASE, WAKE UP!
THE HEAD! NO, PLEASE!!!
ALICE ALICE ALICE ALICE
ALICE... COME ON, ALICE... WAKE UP!
MMMH... YES...
IT LOOKS LIKE YOU WERE SLEEPING DURING THE WHOLE HISTORY LESSON!
NO, OF COURSE NOT!
UMM... THE CATERPILLAR WAS BLOWING BIG SMOKE RINGS...
WHAT ARE YOU TALKING ABOUT?
IT WAS DEFINITELY TH CHESHIRE CA
AND SO ALICE RETURNED HOME... NOT WITHOUT CASTING A GLANCE BEHIND HER...
BUT... WHAT KIND OF STORY IS THAT?! COME ON...
LET'S GO HAVE TEA!
WE'LL HAVE SOME BISCUITS!
... TOWARDS WONDERLAND, WHERE CHILDREN LIVE HAPPILY!
THE END

WRITER
François Corteggiani

ART
Andrea Nicolucci
Sara Storino
Francesco Legramandi

DARK HORSE BOOKS

PRESIDENT AND PUBLISHER **Mike Richardson**

COLLECTION EDITOR **Freddye Miller**   COLLECTION ASSISTANT EDITOR **Judy Khuu**

DESIGNER **Jen Edwards**   DIGITAL ART TECHNICIAN **Samantha Hummer**

Neil Hankerson Executive Vice President • Tom Weddle Chief Financial Officer • Randy Stradley Vice President of Publishing • Nick McWhorter Chief Business Development Officer • Dale LaFountain Chief Information Officer • Matt Parkinson Vice President of Marketing • Cara Niece Vice President of Production and Scheduling • Mark Bernardi Vice President of Book Trade and Digital Sales • Ken Lizzi General Counsel • Dave Marshall Editor in Chief • Davey Estrada Editorial Director • Chris Warner Senior Books Editor • Cary Grazzini Director of Specialty Projects • Lia Ribacchi Art Director • Vanessa Todd-Holmes Director of Print Purchasing • Matt Dryer Director of Digital Art and Prepress • Michael Gombos Senior Director of Licensed Publications • Kari Yadro Director of Custom Programs • Kari Torson Director of International Licensing • Sean Brice Director of Trade Sales

DISNEY PUBLISHING WORLDWIDE GLOBAL MAGAZINES, COMICS AND PARTWORKS

PUBLISHER Lynn Waggoner • EDITORIAL TEAM Bianca Coletti (Director, Magazines), Guido Frazzini (Director, Comics), Carlotta Quattrocolo (Executive Editor), Stefano Ambrosio (Executive Editor, New IP), Camilla Vedove (Senior Manager, Editorial Development), Behnoosh Khalili (Senior Editor), Julie Dorris (Senior Editor), Mina Riazi (Assistant Editor), Gabriela Capasso (Assistant Editor) • DESIGN Enrico Soave (Senior Designer) • ART Ken Shue (VP, Global Art), Manny Mederos (Senior Illustration Manager, Comics and Magazines), Roberto Santillo (Creative Director), Marco Ghiglione (Creative Manager), Stefano Attardi (Illustration Manager) • PORTFOLIO MANAGEMENT Olivia Ciancarelli (Director) • BUSINESS & MARKETING Mariantonietta Galla (Senior Manager, Franchise), Virpi Korhonen (Editorial Manager)

Published by Dark Horse Books
A division of Dark Horse Comics LLC
10956 SE Main Street | Milwaukie, OR 97222

DarkHorse.com

To find a comics shop in your area, visit comicshoplocator.com

First Dark Horse Books edition: March 2020
ISBN 978-1-50671-735-7
Digital ISBN 978-1-50671-744-9

1 3 5 7 9 10 8 6 4 2
Printed in China

The classic tale of
Snow White and the Seven Dwarfs
reawakens!

Relive the beloved Disney fairy tale through the
first-person perspective of Snow White herself!

978-1-50671-462-2 • $12.99